MacDonald Harris is "one of our major novelists" (*Los Angeles Times*), "a thinking man's novelist" (*The New York Times*), a writer whose "work is both sensational and revolutionary" (*Chicago Tribune*) and marked by "intellectual playfulness, numinous sexuality and a disturbing sense of fatalism" (*The Washington Post*). The recipient of an Award in Literature from the American Academy and Institute of Arts and Letters and a Special Achievement Award in Fiction from the PEN Los Angeles Center, Harris lives in Newport Beach, California.

GLOWSTONE

Also by MacDonald Harris

GLOWSTONE

a novel
by

MacDonald Harris

William Morrow and Company, Inc.
New York

Library of Congress Cataloging-in-Publication Data

Harris, MacDonald, 1921–
Glowstone.
I. Title.
PS3558.E458G5   1987   813'.54   86-28612
ISBN 0-688-07049-3

Printed in the United States of America

First Edition

1 2 3 4 5 6 7 8 9 10

BOOK DESIGN BY ARLENE GOLDBERG

For François and Josette

pour ces scènes inoubliables

If you feel yourself glow with love like an ember, I say that you are in great danger, for who can tell the glow of God from that of the Adversary?

—St. Anselm of Turin, XII century

GLOWSTONE

A WORD TO THE READER

At the beginning of Leoncavallo's opera *I Pagliacci*, a costumed figure comes before the audience and sings, "Excuse me if I present myself. I am the Prologue." So do I come before you, a masked figure standing before the curtain in the theater of our drama. The story I have to tell you is one that I know well. It is the story of Claire Savarin-Decker, a Belgian-American woman who worked as a scientist in Paris around the turn of the century. In those days it wasn't the usual thing for women to be scientists, or even to study science in the university. But Claire was exceptional. She made her way against the opposition, and in the end the world accepted her as a distinguished contributor to her field.

She was controversial even in her own time. Some people regarded her as a saint of science, a model for all future women who wished to take their places beside men in the important work of the world; others thought she was a wrongheaded and authoritarian bigot. The charge is also made that in devoting herself to her work in the laboratory she neglected her family, that is her daughter, although I myself am reluctant to blame her on this account. The daughter turned out well enough, so who is interested in whether she was happy as a child? Few children are. Anyhow, Claire's own importance as a scientist was great enough that the question of whether she took proper care of her child was negligible. So argue her admirers.

And as another controversial subject, there is this substance she invented or discovered. It was said to cure all diseases and heal wounds magically; the prophecy was made that in the future it would light the cities of the world and provide the power for its factories, bringing a new Golden Age to mankind. On the other hand it seems that some girls in New England died horribly on account of it. If that story is true, Claire has a great deal to answer for. The question has been asked, if you could kill a Mandarin in China by pressing a button, and by this act become immensely wealthy, and no one would ever know about it, would you do it? Claire, willingly or no, killed her Mandarin. We are all guilty of such things, more or less. If we don't kill a Mandarin, we wish in our secret thoughts to do so. In this respect Claire was no different from anyone, except that the counters she handled in the game of life were more valuable, and more dangerous to others. Since she never confessed her sins to the world, it is up to me to confess them for her. I intend to tell you everything, at least everything I know, and that is a lot. Some parts of it won't be pleasant to tell about. Other parts are delightful. I am looking forward to the task.

In an odd way, if this is to be the story of Claire herself, it must begin with the event that she thought was the end of her life, the death of her husband in 1906. Without this terrible event, she would never have drunk champagne or ridden a bicycle, she would never have picked red currants in the country—these are trivialities of course, but she would never have played out the full drama of her life, she would never have found out who she really was. If God (I believe in Him a little, even though Claire didn't) takes away something with one hand, He often gives us something better with the other. Nothing is aleatory, everything is for some cause and has some purpose.

GLOWSTONE

If I am wrong, then everything is only sound and fury, signifying nothing. I hope that isn't so.

In telling the story of Claire's life, I have to tell a little of my own story too, as you will see in time. I was present at many of the events I have to recount, and I was acquainted with most of the people involved. To my mind, to live in Paris in the time before the Great War was to be one of the most privileged of the billions of people who have been born on this earth. We were different from you in those days. We wore different clothes and sang different songs, and in many ways we were frivolous and perverse. We had our faults, many of them. We were not the first to discover the "fierce desirability of the world," but we surrendered ourselves to it with more than an ordinary fervor. It is for this reason, perhaps, that our time is called the Belle Époque.

If you want to see the scenes of these events you may go and see them today—an old house in the Faubourg St.-Germain, a former surgical theater at 5, Rue de l'École-de-Médecine, a café on the river at Bougival, an old farmhouse, converted to an artist's studio, on the Seine near Vernon. As for the people, they are mostly gone, except for me. Perhaps Onyx Fabre is still alive. Or Carlo Bini; I don't know about him; he went back to his native Bologna before the War. He was not altogether a respectable person, I am afraid. But what I am going to tell you is not whether we were good or bad, but what we did, and why we did it, at least insofar as I can guess about the others. At the end of his aria, the Prologue of *I Pagliacci*, a hunchback in a clown suit, begs us, "And you, rather than our poor mountebanks' costumes, consider our souls, because we are people of flesh and bone, and breathe like you the air of this orphan world." This orphan world; what a mysterious phrase. Do you understand it? I think I do.

The Prologue speaks very well for his fellow comedians, and for the human race, I think. And that is how I would like you to regard us, as people of flesh and bone who breathe the same air as you. We are not fictions, we are humans. And who am I, the teller of the tale? I am the projection of your self into the story. I am the thought you are having as you read this page.

I

When Lancelot came with the news of the accident, Claire was at home in her apartment in Rue François-Villon. Ordinarily she put in the day at work in the laboratory with her husband, Paul, an eminent physicist and director of the Savarin Institute, but today she had come home at noon because she felt a little unwell. Her daughter, who went to a lycée in Avenue Montaigne, was to be let out early because it was a half-holiday. Hermine had not come home yet and Claire was in the kitchen of the apartment, a comfortable, old-fashioned place with large rooms and gray nondescript walls. Although she had a pain in her back and felt weak, she never lay down in the daytime and she didn't do so now. She was dabbling at making herself some lunch when she heard the knock. As soon as she saw Lancelot come through the door followed by Fabre she turned pale.

None of the three spoke for an instant. At last Claire managed to articulate, "It's something in the laboratory?"

"The laboratory?"

"Something has happened at the laboratory?"

"No, Claire. Nothing has happened at the laboratory."

There was another silence. The honest Fabre, the mechanic and general handyman in the laboratory, twisted his cap in his hands.

"But—it's Paul."

Lancelot nodded. "There's been an accident in the street. A tragic—how can I say—" He stopped, at a loss for words. "I'm afraid he is very badly injured indeed. He's been taken to the Hôtel-Dieu."

Claire at first showed no reaction, although it was clear that she understood what he was saying. Lancelot, with as much tact as he could muster, made two points: that according to the doctors there was no hope, and that if she wished to see her dying husband before the end it was necessary to hurry. She nodded, looked around distractedly for her black paletot which she found on a hook on the kitchen door, and scribbled a note for her daughter: Gone to the lab, your lunch is soup on the stove and bread. Then she accompanied Lancelot and Fabre down to the street.

She seemed not at all struck to find the floor of the cab covered with blood, and asked no questions about it; perhaps she didn't notice, or perhaps she guessed the truth without asking: that this was the same cab the police had used to carry the dying man to the hospital, and that Lancelot had then taken it to come to Rue François-Villon to bring her the news. The three of them, crowded in the small vehicle, jolted over the paving stones through a light rain in the direction of the Hôtel-Dieu. Even though Lancelot knew the details of the accident would be painful, he found the silence even more painful. Moved by the terrible drama of the moment, he had an irresistible desire to tell someone what he knew about it, and the only person available was Claire.

"In the morning, as you know, he went to a meeting of the Union of European Scientists in the St.-Germain quarter. He then set off for the office of his publisher Montmorency, on the quay near the Pont-Neuf. It's likely that he was preoccupied with some scientific problem or other, and didn't pay proper attention as he was crossing Rue Dauphine, just by the bridge. It was raining as it is now, and the pavement was slick. He was carrying an umbrella and this no doubt obscured his vision. The witnesses said that he was looking the other way, toward the river, and didn't see the wagon coming down the slope of the street. He fell under the horses and the wheel of the wagon passed over his chest. The wagon was very heavy; it was loaded with military uniforms," he added, not sure why this last detail was significant, but taking a satisfaction in relating all the facts with precision.

Claire nodded. She was still in a numb, unreal, half-inarticulate state. What she felt was a kind of strangeness, an oddness as though her body did not belong to herself, instead of the grief she expected. She had forgotten completely the minor aches and pains that had brought her home from the laboratory. Looking out at the swaying back of the rhythmically trotting horse, she tried to summon up the emotions that were appropriate to the occasion. They were passing the Lycée Buffon and the Hôpital des Enfants Malades, and she gazed out through the rain-blurred window at the familiar buildings. "He asked for me?"

"No. He can't speak. He indicated your photograph, out of the objects the police found in his wallet."

A little later, in Rue de l'Odéon, she asked, "Did he suffer much pain?"

"I'm sorry. As to that I really can't say," said Lancelot.

When they arrived at the Hôtel-Dieu there was a certain amount of confusion. At the wicket of the reception hall Lancelot repeated "Dr. Savarin" several times before he made it clear that he was asking for a patient and not for a member of the hospital staff. Finally they found that a cot had been set up for Paul in a corridor, since for the moment no bed could be found for him in a ward in this large and overcrowded public hospital. Word had spread that the eminent physicist, director of the Savarin Institute in Rue de l'École-de-Médecine, had been admitted with serious injuries, and a cluster of doctors and students was gathered around the cot, from which threads of blood fell slowly to the dark polished floor. They looked around in silence as Lancelot and Claire approached with Fabre following.

"I am Professor Lancelot, Dr. Savarin's colleague at the Institute. And this is Madame Savarin-Decker, his—" he almost said his widow, and checked himself—"his wife."

They drew apart respectfully, still silent. Claire came up to the cot followed by Lancelot and Fabre.

The dying man did not precisely smile, but a look of animation, of interest and satisfaction, came over his tormented face. He nodded, the only gesture that he could perform now that his weakness had made it virtually impossible to move his hands or arms.

"My poor Paul. Have you suffered much?"

He nodded, still with the same expression of animated interest.

She knelt and took his hand, ignoring the blood which covered his body and fell stickily onto her shoes and plain black cloak.

"My poor Paul. My Paul. My Paul."

Paul stared back at her with a wide-eyed but calm intensity. Lancelot, finding this one-sided conversation painful, attempted to inject a more serious and more ceremonious note, one suitable to the tragedy and pathos of the situation, as painful as it was for him to articulate his thoughts in these melancholy circumstances; in short he embarked on a speech, which he was inclined to do on almost any occasion. "That this should happen from—a sheer accident—from a moment of inattention," he murmured to both husband and wife, and to the circle of white-clad watchers. "That such a brilliant mind—that such an extraordinary intelligence—that a genius whose discoveries have already been of inestimable value to mankind, and would surely have continued further—" He broke off, not out of grief but out of a paucity of rhetoric; he quite literally couldn't find his way out of his sentence.

The dying man nodded and managed to raise his hand enough to point to Lancelot. His fellow scientist understood what was meant, that he wished to know what had happened in the laboratory during his absence. "During the morning we continued quantitative analysis of the samples of chloride salts produced yesterday from fractional crystallization. We now estimate the atomic weight at two hundred twenty-eight." Paul nodded and looked away, satisfied.

Then he seemed to think of something else. As they watched a look of alarm, of half-forgotten and then remembered dread, formed gradually over the tortured face. With a prodigious effort, one that caused his entire body to tremble, he managed to raise both hands from the bloodstained cot. A young doctor moved forward to restrain him, but was halted by his superior. Facing directly toward his wife, with a look of terrible intensity, Dr. Savarin raised his hands with palms outward, like a saint showing the Stigmata. The doctors, gazing curiously at this gesture, noticed something about the hands that surely could have nothing to do with the accident in Rue Dauphine. The fingertips were blackened and creased with the signs of half-healed ulcers. Farther up, the fingers to the first and second joints were red and inflamed, and at one point on the right forefinger a whitish crack exuded a trace of serum. Dr. Savarin nodded, a gesture which now gave him the air of a sage and all-seeing even though suffering prophet. He looked directly at Claire. He nodded. And pointed first to his own crushed chest. And then to her. I. And you.

What did he mean? Lancelot turned to Fabre perplexed, and the doctors whispered together. Only Claire stood calmly, gazing at the dying man with a fixity which seemed to absorb her completely and to exclude all external stimulus or distraction, even all thought. Did she understand what he meant? No one could tell; even she herself was not sure. Her own fingers bore the same scars and lesions. They were unimportant, Paul had told her a hundred times; simply a discomfort that went with working in the laboratory, like the acid burns which are the distinguishing marks of all chemists.

Dr. Savarin nodded one last time. Then he managed to smile, a curious and significant rictus which he held for a few moments, still looking directly at Claire. He died a few minutes later, without having spoken a word from the time he fell under the horses' hooves in Rue Dauphine.

Accompanied by Lancelot, Claire now had the painful task of returning to the apartment in Rue François-Villon and telling Hermine that her father was dead. Without a word, Lancelot at her elbow, she set out for the omnibus stop at the Pont-Neuf. Why an omnibus? Perhaps she had been affected more than she showed by the blood in the cab that brought her to the Hôtel-Dieu. Of course that one was gone, dismissed with charges paid by the efficient and compassionate Lancelot, but they could have taken another; there was a queue of them waiting in Rue de la Cité by the hospital. The reason she took the omnibus had nothing to do with the horror of that other black vehicle with its carpet of darkling red under their feet. It was simply that she knew Hermine would stay in the apartment until she got home, and so there was plenty of time. Cabs, to her mind, were only for extraordinary circumstances. It was an extraordinary circumstance if one's husband was killed in a street accident, but once he was dead, there was nothing extraordinary about coming home afterwards; it was simply what one did as a matter of course. Taking the omnibus was what Paul himself would have done, she told herself in a piece of twisted logic she did not quite follow herself. In another part of her mind, she knew that she didn't want to get home too soon, dreading the interview with her daughter whom she only half understood and was a little afraid of. Distracted by the shock of what had happened, she was not thinking clearly and wanted above all to continue in her usual daily habits, the habits of times before this terrible blow had struck; and she always went by omnibus, never by cab. And so had Paul, in fact he preferred to walk when the distances were not too great. His austerity, which was part and parcel of his devotion to science, was the most visible and outstanding quality of his character. And it had become her austerity too, since her own life and personality had become so intertwined with his from the day she married him, he already an eminent scientist, she only a student of twenty. And now he was no more! She sat in the omnibus grimly watching the familiar shops passing by, now oddly transformed, become magic or fiendish in a curious way, as though things were speaking to her in a voice so low she couldn't catch the words, only the menacing and ironic tone of their discourse. Lancelot sat respectfully at her elbow. If he had any opinions about taking an omnibus under these circumstances he didn't express them.

Since the omnibus stopped frequently to take on and discharge passengers, it was a trip of over forty minutes from the Pont-Neuf to the corner where Claire and Lancelot descended in Rue de Vaugirard. It was about three o'clock. Still in silence, they walked the short distance to the apartment in Rue François-Villon. Passing the loge of the concièrge, Claire went up the stairs to the landing and opened the door of the apartment. Inside, Hermine appeared framed in the doorway at the other end of the room.

Hermine was sixteen, a slim grave child with dark eyes and a thatch of hair falling in a fringe over her forehead. When she heard the key in the lock she had stopped in the doorway of the kitchen. Then, when her mother came through the door followed by Lancelot, she remained standing where she was, frozen, with a bite of cheese and bread she had taken a moment before lodged motionless in her mouth.

"My poor Hermine," said Claire.

"What is it, Maman?"

Claire moved across the room to embrace her. "My poor, poor Hermine."

The two women remained clutched together awkwardly for a moment or two. They had hardly ever embraced since Hermine was a small child.

"Is it Papa?"

Claire drew away from her daughter and regarded her intently, pursing up her mouth in an effort to prevent it from trembling. "Hermine, Hermine. As you know, your father is somewhat absentminded and sometimes doesn't take proper precautions."

"Was it in the laboratory?"

Claire reflected, with something like a sad inward smile, that this was exactly how she had responded when Lancelot came bearing his news only two hours before, with this same question and this same initial lack of grief. Perhaps she and Hermine were more alike than she thought, or perhaps her daughter's question was only the natural one that anyone would ask. She told her, still trying to maintain a calm expression, "It was not in the laboratory. There was an accident. Your father is very badly injured."

Hermine stared at her, and now inexplicably she began to chew. Her jaws moved slowly and rhythmically while she stared with unblinking fixity, with a terrible calm, at her mother. But Claire saw that Hermine's eyes were not fixed on her face. Instead her gaze had come to rest at a spot on her black paletot just below her shoulder. Claire bent to look at the place, could not see it, and raised her fingers to touch it. It was moist and sticky. She looked at her fingers. She hadn't noticed it, but the blood from Paul's chest had touched her when she bent to kiss him.

"Why do you tell me he is injured?" said Hermine, still chewing but now setting down the bread and cheese on a table. "He is dead."

"My poor Hermine."

"How? *How?*"

Lancelot felt absolutely obliged to intervene. The scene was painful. "There was an unfortunate accident in the street. In Rue Dauphine, just by the quays. In crossing the street, Dr. Savarin slipped and fell under a wagon. He was taken to the Hôtel-Dieu but nothing could be done for him. He died peaceably."

"The how is not important, my dear," said Claire softly.

More than ever before she felt separated by a mysterious gulf from her daughter. There was the matter of her continuing to chew her mouthful of bread and cheese while she was informed of the death of her father. Of course, it had been in her mouth before she, Claire, opened the door, and that being so, she had only two choices, either to remove the glutinous mass or to chew it and swallow it. Claire saw this with a scientific clarity. Still it was strange the way the girl behaved, as though she hardly grasped what was told her and was angry at her, at her mother, for attempting to break the news gently. And this emotion on her daughter's part was so irrational, and so human, that Claire was filled with love for her, with a wild and fearful possessiveness. She stepped forward and embraced her again, this time gripping her so that their two bodies were pressed together along their entire lengths. Her frame trembled, so violently that it made Hermine tremble too. When Claire spoke she had surrendered herself finally to tears; her voice was broken and inarticulate. "My Hermine, you were your father's child, he loved you more than any person on earth"— more than herself, she realized she was saying senselessly— "and he was for you the light who brought you all grace, all charity and security, he was the meaning in your life, just as he was for me, and for all of those who shared his work. And now he is gone, and so you and I must love each other the more. We must come to know each other as we have not before, we must become intimate, we must seek through our love for each other to fill the terrible gulf that has been left in our lives by the death of your father, and my husband. My lover, for I never loved another."

All this she got out in a strangled difficult voice, her arms gripping and releasing her daughter in the rhythm of the words she was reciting, as though Hermine had become for her some strange instrument like a bagpipe which she was attempting to play as she spoke. Hermine's own emotions were tumultuous. She felt shock and grief at her father's death, but she was repelled by this new and reckless, previously unknown passion of her mother, which seemed to have something sensual in it, a deep corporeal need which she had never expressed before even to Papa, at least not in the presence of Hermine. It was all the worse in that she felt the unmistakable stirrings in herself of an erotic response to her mother's embrace. She had discovered a strange and important fact, one little discussed even among adults, that great grief, or any great emotion, is aphrodisiac. It was the first time that Hermine had taken notice of this particular sensation in herself. She extricated herself and, echoing her mother's rudimentary expostulation, murmured, "My poor Maman," several times. She caught sight of the half-eaten bread and cheese on the table and wondered if she might take another bite of it. Probably not, at least until her mother went into the bedroom to be alone with her grief. And would she go to school tomorrow? In the case of the death of someone, there would be arrangements to be made, although she wasn't sure what they were. She needed to know, since if she was going she had lessons to prepare.

Claire looked at her daughter. In spite of her grief, which made everything about her fuzzy and unclear, she glimpsed something on Hermine's face which made her suspect that as soon as she left the room the girl would go back to eating her unfinished bread and cheese. She turned and found Lancelot regarding her, awkwardly and with some embarrassment, from his position just inside the door of the apartment. His hat was in his hands and he chewed his lip thoughtfully.

"My dear Lancelot, how kind you've been, and how difficult it would be to get through all of this without your help. How can I thank you. You've been like an angel to us today, an angel of grief it is true, but a valuable one, without whom we could hardly have borne our burden."

"But I beg you, Claire. I was as deeply shocked as you were at the loss of our dear colleague. We're old friends after all. I've known you both for years." He spoke in his perfect French which she had always envied. Her own French had a Belgian accent and was contaminated as well by the twang of her American father. Even Paul's French bore the trace of his Alsatian origin, but Lancelot's was flawless. It was strange, she always thought of him as Lancelot, simply by his last name, and was scarcely aware of his given name. Now she remembered that it was Paul, the same as her husband's. It was very curious that this had never struck her before. Grief shook up all the ventricles and chambers of the brain, she thought, bringing to light memories, shadows, obscure connections that had rested somewhere in the bottom of the consciousness, things you never knew were there. She realized that he was still speaking and made an effort to focus on his words, banishing all these darkling and intangible wisps which were quite inconsistent with her way of thinking before the shock of the tragedy. He was saying, "The practical details that must be seen to in the next few days are tedious and often painful. If you could see fit to charge me with the arrangements—"

"Arrangements?"

"For the obsequies of our dear colleague."

She smiled, feeling even in her pain that there was a new beauty in her calm, or more precisely, in the dignity and grace with which she now managed to surmount her grief, after her excessive display of emotion when she had embraced Hermine.

"Of course. It would be very kind of you. I have no experience of such things and I'm not French. I don't know what is done. I wish only that the ceremony should be simple and without ostentation. Paul would have wanted it so."

"Quite. Please allow me to take everything on myself. As for you, Claire, you must rest. I've noticed that you've seemed tired lately. You're perhaps not entirely in good health. You and Hermine must seek consolation in your love for each other"— did he allow a slight irony to creep in as he said this? He himself wasn't sure. He had noticed the intensity and oddness of the embrace between the two women, and he didn't approve— "and economize your forces for the difficult days that lie ahead. Please don't concern yourself with the laboratory. I'll call there this afternoon to inform everybody what has happened, and to make arrangements for the work to continue on at least a contingent basis."

"I'm grateful for your concern, and your help." She offered her hand—as she moved toward him he was alarmed for an instant, thinking that she might embrace him as she had her daughter—and he pressed it briefly, deciding at the last moment to bow and bend his lips within a centimeter of it and then withdraw.

"In this moment of grief for us all, believe me, Claire, your very faithful and humble servant"—he was actually speaking to her as though he were writing a letter! "Good-bye then. Leave everything to me."

She remained fixed where she was, and he shut the door of

the apartment behind him and hurried down the stair. In Rue Vaugirard he set off on foot for the center of the city but soon saw a cab passing and flagged it. He could hardly afford it, but this was not an ordinary day; he was back at the laboratory in Rue de l'École-de-Médecine in a quarter of an hour. Whatever had possessed the woman to take the omnibus back to her apartment! His intense admiration for Claire was tempered with annoyance. She must have been distracted by the blow that had struck her. The omnibus, leaving the Pont-Neuf, had gone directly up Rue Dauphine past the spot where her husband had been crushed by the wagon. He had been unable to avoid staring at the place on the pavement, but she seemed to notice nothing. He didn't remember whether anyone had told her the exact spot where the accident had happened, and in any case the rain would have washed away the blood. It had struck him as curious, as the omnibus had passed the spot, that the cluster of spectators had disappeared, that no one lingered to look at the fateful place on the pavement, that a man from a paints-and-oil shop at the scene of the accident was calmly sweeping off his sidewalk with a broom of rushes, that no one had yet put up a plaque on the wall: *Here on May 10, 1906 was fatally injured the eminent Paul Savarin, Docteur ès Sciences, Director of the Savarin Institute, recipient of the Gold Medal of the Royal Academy, Doctor Honoris Causa of Cambridge University.*

On the day of the burial in the Cimetière Montparnasse the rain had stopped but the skies were still leaden. A considerable cortège, longer than Claire or anyone else had expected, trailed through the streets from the church of St.-Julian-le-Pauvre to the entrance of the cemetery in the Boulevard Raspail, where it stopped while the occupants of the vehicles descended. A number of carriages were empty: those representing several professors of the Sorbonne, which had snubbed Paul's scientific work and never admitted him to a professorship, the Rector of the University, and the President of the Academy of Sciences. From the gateway the mourners made their way on foot to the graveside at the west end of the cemetery, not far from the tomb of Baudelaire. There they gathered, forming a considerable crowd that blocked the alleys and paths, as many as possible crowding under a canopy of black canvas trimmed with white erected by the cemetery authorities. The women were in somber clothes, for the most part black, the men in black and most of them wearing shiny top hats—Hermine had never seen so many chapeaux haut-de-forme; they blossomed like strange black flowers in the green expanse of the cemetery.

Claire, jumbled and pressed in this unaccustomed crowd of people, supported on one side by her daughter and the other by Lancelot, was hardly aware of what was happening except that a voice was mumbling from the graveside and that a large and ornate casket, far too expensive she was sure, sat next to the grave with floral wreathes and horseshoes almost covering it. She caught sight of a ribbon stamped "To the Glory of the Republic," a slogan which she found incomprehensible. On another, one of the few she could read in the mass of flowers, she made out the word "Cambridge"; the wreath was no doubt from the fellows and students of Kings College, who had acclaimed Paul so warmly when he received his honorary degree only two years before.

In the crowd of mourners she saw her fellow workers from the laboratory—Delvaux the spectroscopist, Carlo Bini, the young Swiss woman Délicienne Maedl, the handyman Onyx Fabre. They seemed strange to her, like actors playing the parts of people she knew in the real world. Even her own daughter by her side, even the faithful Lancelot, shared this quality of painted actors in a theater, of something unreal and false, a trick intended to deceive her about the true nature of what was going on in this strange and parklike place with its slabs of granite and its odd miniature houses with grillwork doors. The mumbling from the graveside continued. What on earth was the priest saying with all his mumbo jumbo? It went on endlessly. An acolyte handed him a receptacle from which he sprinkled holy water on the casket. The flowers were removed, as Claire looked on through a haze that perhaps came from some condition of the atmosphere peculiar to cemeter-

ies, and the far too expensive casket was lowered into the pit
in the earth with an apparatus that Claire had never even heard
about and had perhaps only dreamed of as a child—the canvas straps were paid out by cranks, which in turn were con-
trolled by ratchets that made a sound like cicadas in a field on
a hot afternoon. Claire was invited to sprinkle a handful of
earth into the open grave before it was sealed. She attempted
to do so, but another impulse struck her and she flung it instead over the spectators. There was a small scandal; people
whispered, the officiating priest looked at her severely, and
she was led away by Hermine to the carriage waiting at the
graveled entrance to the cemetery.

It was late at night and Hermine was safely in bed; the sym-
pathetic friends and colleagues had long gone away, having
consumed the exiguous two bottles of wine and single plate of
little iced cakes that Claire had provided. (*She is an incredible
miser, that one,* suggested a voice. And another: *Just like him.*)
The last omnibus of the evening—they ran only until midnight—set Claire down in the Carrefour de l'Odéon, and she
made her way out of the square into the almost deserted Rue
de l'École-de-Médecine. In the inky darkness of the courtyard
she fitted her key into the lock and swung open the door to
the laboratory. The large room, formerly a surgical theater of
the Medical School, had been fitted with electricity since 1896
but she had no need to turn it on; she knew her way among
the tables and instrument stands by heart, and besides there
was another source of illumination in the laboratory.

It was apparent only if the room was totally dark, as it was
now. From a half-dozen different places in the laboratory there
came a faint bluish-green glow, silvery at the edges, confusing
the eyesight so that its boundaries were not quite clear, seem-
ing to tremor at the center in the way of a flame even in a
room without drafts. From a horizontal tube connected to a
gas-exhausting apparatus came a glow more intense than the
others, a light strong enough that it cast a shadow if a piece of
paper was put before it and a finger or a match between them.
In this tube was the product of their years of research in its

purest form, the chloride salt of which Lancelot had spoken to Paul in his dying moments. The phosphorescence from it and the other containers illuminated the room with a faint nocturnal shimmer, making everything seem necromantic, like the chamber of a medieval alchemist.

Glowstone, she said softly to herself, or thought in her mind.

She had hoped the word would console her in her grief, or offer some ray of light to guide her in the future. But it had lost its usual power to enchant her. She felt a new atmosphere gather around her, chill and inexplicably menacing. The dimly lit room seemed to speak with a portent that was all the more disquieting in its total silence. The familiar beakers and caldrons were transformed; they had turned into instruments of a perilous magic, a force which had been friendly and had all at once turned inimical, as though a beloved companion had removed a mask and revealed himself as an adversary. The laboratory was no longer the familiar place where she had worked at the side of Paul; it had become an Etruscan funereal chamber filled with strange ritual instruments.

Now her grief struck her once again with its violence. But this time it did not take the form of tears. A vast wildness swept through her, cleansing and purifying her thoughts like a wind blowing papers from a street. She heard a thin keening that she recognized as coming from her own vocal cords even though she was not conscious of making it. It was a deep primordial lament, not for Paul—that was a personal grief which she had expressed in that brief moment of embracing Hermine, and in the ceremony at the graveside—but for the memory of their work together in the laboratory, a devotion to their craft that had all the powers of a sacrament, a communion that had evoked from nature the gift of this glowing Eucharist in the tube before her. It was a cult that was now dead as the cult of the ancient gods was dead, crushed under a wagon and buried in a hole in the Cimetière Montparnasse, along with her own soul and life which for eighteen years had been a life totally devoted to science.

I shall carry on. I shall carry on with Paul's ghost at my shoulder. Claire didn't turn on the lights, although the switch was only a pace from her hand at a place she knew perfectly. The laboratory was illuminated only by the light from the glowstone samples. She was aware of another sound, which she identified as her own breathing. I have grown very strange in the three days since he is gone, she thought. How close we all are to the animals. Was man an animal or a god? It was a question to be investigated, perhaps by the scientists, perhaps by someone else like the poets. Or, she thought, forgetting for the moment, she might ask Paul. When she realized that this was not possible, she no longer felt any grief, only a sense of isolation in which her soul was in danger of being swept away into an empty cosmos.

We were Paul and Claire. Now he is no more. I am Claire.

The meaning of this cryptic formula, which she repeated over to herself several times like a child trying to memorize it, still eluded her understanding. Perhaps she would grasp it later. With a final look at the darkened laboratory she made her way through the worktables to the door at the end. It opened onto a courtyard enclosed by a wall, with the porter's small lodge at one side. She was careful to lock the door of the laboratory, then she let herself out through the gate, which she unlocked and locked with another key. Now she stood in Rue de l'École-de-Médecine, deserted at this hour except for the passing of an occasional milk wagon or the step of a policeman in his cloak and képi. No more omnibuses; it was after midnight. For a moment she was bewildered. *How is it that I am in Paris? I am only a schoolgirl in Brussels, memorizing Latin declensions and blackening my fingers in the chemistry class with silver nitrate.* This strangeness would follow after her and haunt her, she imagined, for a period of time until she grew used to living in the world without Paul. Even though she was a schoolgirl and knew nothing of Paris, she was able to follow her way easily, with the unconsciousness of long habit, down the inky black street to the Carrefour de l'Odéon. She would have to walk home but she was used to that. Something illuminated the darkness for her, in the secret recesses of her mind; it seemed to her that the air of the city itself was permeated with a thin bluish-green luminescence.

II

Claire Savarin-Decker was born in Brussels in 1868. Her father, Louis P. Decker, was an American mining engineer who was sent by Belgian mining interests to investigate the copper ores of the Congo, later to become the basis of the vast Belgian empire in Africa. At that time he was still a young man. After his report was presented he decided to stay on in Brussels, since he was getting on well with his Belgian employers and was well paid by them. A year or so later he met Émilie de Verhaeren, a young woman of prominent family who came from St.-Amand, near Antwerp, and was studying art at the Conservatory. They were married after only a month of courtship; Émilie was carried away, not by the young American's passion—because he seemed totally passionless—but by the sheer force of his will, his cool efficient way of setting out to get anything he wanted in the world. The Verhaeren family were impressed by his wealth—he had already accumulated investments to keep him in comfort all his life—and by his modest, austere, and self-contained character. Why Louis was attracted to Émilie was less clear, but she had a reputation as a famous beauty, spoke four languages with precision, and was not without talent as an artist. Their daughter Claire was born a little less than a year after their marriage, and a son, Georges, two years later. Mme Decker's womb was damaged by this second childhood and there were no more children.

Claire grew up in a pleasant suburb of Brussels, with the forest of Soignies near at hand, on a street of fashionable villas and country houses. Her childhood was unremarkable except that she was an exceptionally quiet child, undemonstrative and undemanding. She was a good student, willing at helping with the housework, and a devoted reader; however she wasn't interested in novels and read mainly biography, letters, history, and natural philosophy, as it was called in those days. The science she discovered in these books seemed to her not so much a description of the real world as a form of fascinating and complex fiction; she had never seen chloride, mutations, or inertia and had no idea that these things were all about her in her daily existence.

When she was fourteen she was enrolled in an academy for young ladies in the fashionable Quartier Louis, in the Upper Town of Brussels. The Académie Ferney was conducted on progressive and modern lines, particularly in its science courses, less so in the arts (the reading of novels was forbidden). It was the first girls' school in Europe to install chemistry and physics laboratories where genuine research could be done. At fifteen, Claire had already discovered a previously unknown quality of titanium—that it formed odd copperlike crystals when heated with cyanide in a vacuum. In her careful schoolgirl hand she wrote a paper on her findings with the help of her teacher, Amato Desiato, a kindly and untalented Italian who was fond of young girls and had sacrificed whatever scientific career he might have had to spend his life teaching at the Académie Ferney. Since in those days it was not fashionable for young ladies to submit articles to scientific journals, the article appeared under Professor Desiato's signature. Thus the Deckers had no idea that their daughter was working with something so dangerous as cyanide at the school they had so carefully chosen for her.

Claire, who was not interested in boys, gowns, or balls, had discovered the passion of her life: the world of the laboratory with its beakers, retorts, and mysterious blue flames. As a child she had believed that the facts of science applied to a different world; now she discovered that they were a complicated and precise explanation of the everyday world about her, and she lost all interest in any other explanation of this world, those provided by literature, for example, or by religion. Since science took the entire universe for its domain, and had already discovered the secrets of a large part of this universe, there was no reason to trouble oneself over what the priests or poets had to say about the matter. At school she devoted herself almost exclusively to her work in the laboratory; she scanted her Latin and was adept only in French and English, since her family was bilingual. At eighteen, when she left the Académie Ferney, she already bore on her fingers the acid scars and black nitrate stains of the professional chemist.

"She is brilliant. Brilliant," Professor Desiato told her parents, pressing his fingertips together and hardly able to contain himself in his enthusiasm. "Un'intelligenza magnifica! She must go to the university. I have never had a young lady from my classes go on to the university, but she must be the first."

Louis was a little startled. He had known of Claire's high marks in chemistry, but it had never occurred to him that a woman might be a scientist, any more than she might be an engineer like himself. However he had an open mind. "You mean here in Brussels, I imagine. Or in Louvain."

"Ah no. To Paris. To the Sorbonne," Desiato insisted, still making Italian gestures and waving his arm to the west, to the intellectual and cultural capital of Europe. "I will write letters. I am not," he told them, "without acquaintances in the science faculty, even though I am only an humble professor of lycée. To Paris! To Paris she must go!"

"She is only eighteen," murmured Émilie.

"Everything is supervised! Female students are closely looked after by the faculty," said Desiato, inventing this totally, since he knew nothing whatsoever about the matter. "She must go to Paris!"

Émilie and Louis looked at each other, and Louis shrugged.

Neither of them had any feminist notions, but since their second child, Georges, showed no talent for schoolwork, they were willing to support Claire in whatever she chose to do, and they had the means to send her to any university in the world.

As it happened her education cost them nothing. With the strong recommendation of Professor Desiato, and with his discreet disclosure that his titanium paper was actually based on work done nine-tenths by her, she had no trouble getting admitted to the Faculty of Sciences at the Sorbonne and winning a handsome scholarship. When she and her father sat down to discuss her allowance, she surprised him by insisting on living on the scholarship, which was supposed to be adequate to maintain the average student in good health, if not in comfort, in a Paris boardinghouse. From the day she left for the university she was financially independent of her family.

She settled into a rented room in the Latin Quarter and applied herself with a feverish devotion to her studies. Her fellow students in the Faculty of Sciences were of course all men; there was only one other woman, a mustached freak from the South of France named Jenny Lascaux with whom she never exchanged a word. She soon caught the attention of old Professor Puisson-Lepuy, whose field was the rare earths and especially lanthanum, which he had helped to discover. The fact that this element has no qualities and can scarcely be distinguished from aluminum was fitting, since Professor Puisson-Lepuy too had no qualities and was now in his old age only a stocky old gentleman with a head of white hair, obtuse and harmless, a placid ox among the foxes and wolves of the rest of the faculty. He had a stock of platitudinous facts about science which he repeated in his lectures by rote; like many professors he had ended by reciting his own textbooks to his students.

For some reason he took a fancy to Claire. Perhaps, like Desiato, he was fond of young girls, but this seemed unlikely, since in those days Claire was a plain girl without any discernible appeal to the opposite sex. In any case, he sponsored her and encouraged her in her studies, and when she finished her degree he recommended her for a post as assistant in the laboratory of his former student Paul Savarin, who was doing work on the electrochemical properties of Stockhausen earth.

Claire's world was transformed for the second time. The first was when she discovered science and accepted it as an incomplete but infallible explanation for everything that was. The second was when she encountered Paul Savarin.

At that time she was barely twenty-one. He was thirty-four but already one of the most talked-about and controversial scientists in France. In his mid-twenties, as an assistant in the School of Mines, he discovered that the tailings of uranium ore from a refinery in Transylvania caused an electroscope to discharge, showing that they were radiating an unknown energy into the atmosphere. This couldn't be accounted for by a residue of uranium in the tailings; the ore from the mines was a hundred times more active than uranium itself.

He soon resigned from his position at the School of Mines to set up his own laboratory in rooms donated by the Theosophical Society in Rue Gay-Lussac. The University offered him no support and would have nothing to do with his work. Savarin had unorthodox beliefs: that the table of elements was not fixed and immutable, that new elements might be discovered, and that the uranium residue he studied, gradually giving off its energy over thousands of years, might in the end be converted to some other substance such as lead. These theories of the transmutation of elements, the Sorbonne professors contended, were simply a revival of the follies of the medieval alchemists, who had believed that base metals could be converted to silver and gold.

Undeterred by this criticism and by the refusal of financial support, Savarin moved with his apparatus and two assistants into rooms in Rue Gay-Lussac. He began his work with hundred-gram samples of the Stockhausen earth, as it was called from the mine where it was first discovered. Eventually he worked with tons. When he removed the bismuth and the plutonium the samples were still active. Eventually he obtained a solution nine hundred times more active than uranium. What could be the source of this mysterious and apparently infinite energy? He concluded that it was a previously unknown element, probably allied to the rare earth group. He tentatively called the new element S-metal, for Stockhausen.

His fellow worker Jean Delvaux, who joined his staff shortly after the move to the Theosophical Society, was an expert in spectroscopy. He took a tiny drop of the solution from Savarin's beakers and painted it on the electrodes of his apparatus. When he examined the spectrogram he found a new line not identified with any previously known element. But the Sorbonne was still skeptical; the more the evidence suggested that Savarin was right, the more the professors became entrenched in their conservatism. His findings were refused by established journals and he printed them at his own expense as monographs.

Savarin began to suspect that the new element might have medical powers. A boil on Delvaux's hand, which had come from an infection on a holiday, quickly disappeared after exposure to the concentrated salts. He sent specimens to the Ministry of Health and the Army Medical Corps, and the preliminary word came back that the emanations from the samples seemed to have an effect on certain tumors. Savarin was interviewed by a reporter for the popular press, and was quoted as saying that S-metal, when further refined, might prove to be a panacea for a range of diseases from cancer to arthritis. This too annoyed the Sorbonne faculty, joined now by their medical colleagues, and there were more attacks in scientific journals. The controversy was widely reported by the tabloids and Sunday supplements, with artists' depictions of Savarin in his laboratory, something in the style of illustrations for Jules Verne novels. The more he became a popular celebrity, the more he was regarded as a pariah by the authorities of the Sorbonne.

On that day when Claire first presented herself in Rue Gay-Lussac, she found the laboratory at the rear of the building, facing onto a dusty courtyard. She stole in timidly through the unlatched door, looked about in the room in which nobody paid any attention to her, and finally identified the bearded figure of Savarin himself weighing something in the scales.

"I'm Claire Decker."

He finished entering the reading in his log, then he turned. "I've never heard of you."

"Professor Puisson-Lepuy recommended me."

"Ah yes, the Belgian girl. Puisson-Lepuy, you know, is the only professor of the Sorbonne who doesn't think I'm a charlatan."

"I'm half American. Professor Puisson-Lepuy has a great respect for you."

"This is Delvaux, our spectroscopist."

A tall and aloof man in a spotless laboratory coat—Savarin's own was stained with acid marks—offered her his hand without smiling. She was introduced as well to Épinasse, who was in charge of the preliminary refinement of the ore in the caldrons, a harmless ape of a man, hairy and taciturn; and to Bloch, the middle-aged Belgian who at that time served as mechanic and handyman. This was the whole staff of the laboratory.

After the introductions were over Savarin took a few minutes to show her around the laboratory. She hardly dared to look directly at him. Now and then she stole a sidelong glance at the ascetic figure in his stained laboratory coat, his short beard the same color and texture as his hair which was lightly gray like a wolf. Behind the round steel spectacles his eyes flickered from her to the various pieces of apparatus he was showing. When he spoke his voice was low and calm, yet with a note of the portentous like that of an officiating priest.

"You're aware of the work we are doing?"

She nodded, although she knew only the little that Professor Puisson-Lepuy had told her.

"After several years of work, we've succeeded in reducing a ton of Stockhausen ore to five grams of refined material. The electroactive element in it is highly condensed."

Going to the worktable, he charged a gold-leaf electroscope with a glass rod rubbed with silk, a procedure she was familiar with from her classes at the Sorbonne. Inside the bell jar the gold leaves sprang apart in an inverted Y.

Now he unlocked a cabinet and took from it a tiny glass tube containing a sample of refined Stockhausen earth. Holding this in tongs, he touched it to the glass cover of the electroscope. The gold leaves seemed to weaken and falter, then they collapsed.

"The emanations from S-metal have the power to make air conduct electricity. Thus the charge inside the glass bell is dispersed into the atmosphere."

"The sample is radiating something into the atmosphere?"

"Yes."

"And where does the energy come from?"

"No one is sure, Mademoiselle Decker. Perhaps you could help us find out."

There was perhaps a slight irony here. Her question was a naive one, even with a touch of the trivial. But he showed nothing in his manner. She soon learned not to ask so many questions, to keep her eyes and ears open, and to do the work that was assigned her. She seemed to find favor in his eyes. At least he didn't dismiss her after a week, as he had several other assistants sent him by the Sorbonne.

After that first meeting it was a month or more before he addressed a personal remark to her, or spoke to her about anything more than the work of the laboratory. In fact it was she who broke down this formal reserve between them through a blunder that she afterwards remembered with embarrassment. Looking back over her shoulder as she was weighing something in the scales, she unthinkingly called him by his first name. "Paul, should I weigh to three places or is two enough?" Afterwards it seemed to her that she must have called him this in her reveries, in her secret thoughts, so that the fatal syllable slipped out inadvertently when she spoke.

She was flustered but he didn't correct her. He sat at the table for a moment silent after he had answered her question. Then he said, "You know, the first I heard of you was years ago, when I read your paper on titanium."

"My paper?" She looked at him incomprehendingly. "But—it was signed by Professor Desiato."

"That's so. But he confessed that it was your work when he

wrote recommending you to the faculty for your scholarship. Since I'm not distinguished enough to be a member of the faculty, it was Puisson-Lepuy who told me about it."

"How very generous of him."

"Desiato also wrote that you were an angel." He paused and seemed to reflect. "What do you suppose he meant by that?"

Again she was flustered. "I have no idea."

"I doubt if you're an angel," he said, still perfectly serious. He seemed to consider her further. "However, you seem to be a very capable laboratory assistant. Probably the world has more need of those than of angels."

"No doubt," she murmured.

Since he had interrupted his own work, he suggested that she might give him the data from her morning's work so he could enter it in his log. She got out her work sheets, but instead they went on chatting. They were only centimeters apart, sitting on the bench before the acid-stained wooden table. His liquid and agile eyes looked at her with a kind of cautious speculation. He never laughed and he never smiled broadly enough to show his teeth, which were in poor condition because he neglected to brush them. Other men, she thought, looked at her body when they noticed her for the first time; he kept his eyes fixed on her face.

"As a woman," he asked her, "did you find it difficult working as a science student at the Sorbonne?"

"Not particularly. There was another one," she told him, remembering the unhappy and mustached Jenny Lascaux that she had never spoken to.

"There never has been a woman scientist in France. Perhaps there could be one." He seemed to speculate. "No one knows. No one really knows," he went on, "what the difference is between men and women."

She stared at him, and after a moment he smiled, the first time she had seen him do this. Perhaps he was embarrassed at the innuendo he had strayed into. He actually blushed a little. Claire sensed that a good feeling was in the air, like the mute understanding of two timid animals.

Another man at this point might have asked her out to a

café; the Boulevard St.-Michel was only a few steps away. He presented her with a gift far more wonderful. "Here's the log. Why don't you enter your morning's data for yourself." He passed her the laboratory log, which nobody but himself had ever touched.

They were married a little over six months later. For the civil ceremony at the Mairie of the Sixth Arrondissement she bought a simple black dress from the Bon Marché, an affair of serge with short sleeves and not an item of decoration except a black-on-black embroidery on the military collar which fastened with a snap. Paul was in a frock coat with a white wing collar, a rig which he must have borrowed, since she never saw it again for the rest of his life. The witnesses were Puisson-Lepuy and Paul's married sister Evaline. As it happened the day was Claire's birthday, the twenty-sixth of August, but this was a total coincidence and she didn't mention it to Paul; it was the clerk who pointed it out when he entered the names in the register. Although Claire didn't believe there was anything fatal about coincidences, she felt this one was fitting; it was a rebirth for her, the first step in a totally new life. Following the ceremony she and Paul went to Bougival, on the Seine not far from Paris, to spend the weekend in a quiet hotel. They were back at work in the laboratory on Monday.

Since Claire at this time lived in lodgings and Paul with his married sister, they had to look about for another place to live. In the meanwhile they kept to their old arrangements; it was a month or so before they found a suitable apartment. Even to Claire this seemed an odd way of being married; they met every day in the laboratory, just as before, and went home in the evening, she to her student room and he to his sister's apartment in Place des Victoires. Sometimes they had dinner together at the Bouillon Duval in the Latin Quarter, among students and workmen. It occurred to her to wonder why they hadn't set about finding an apartment earlier before they were married. Yet she found that she hardly missed the lovemaking into which Paul had introduced her in the hotel in Bougival. It was as though it had not really happened, as though it had taken place in a dream or another existence. It was not that she hadn't enjoyed it, although she had *not* enjoyed it exactly; the question of enjoyment didn't enter into her sensations. It was a mystery that he somehow made scientific, as he did everything. He introduced her into the mysteries of the flesh in the way he might have shown her some chemical reaction, a precipitation of crystals of an unusual color, with the air of demonstrating a process known to him but not to her. It was all the same, love and science were part of the same wisdom of the universe, a knowledge that he possessed to a commanding degree, and she as yet only partly.

After they found their apartment in Rue François-Villon, near the Abattoirs—a modest and inexpensive neighborhood, but a respectable one, as he was quick to point out—these conjugal rites resumed, and Claire found them even more mysterious and improbable than she had remembered. It was as though one inserted a bar of iron into a beaker of quicksilver and both elements were transformed, growing heated and exciting each other, emitting strange rays, each transformed into something that was no longer iron and no longer quicksilver but a new element which existed only in the presence of the other. That bodies behaved in this way wasn't to be doubted. It was an observable fact and therefore a scientific one, and one in which Claire took a considerable interest. But she still remained chiefly interested in those reactions the two of them observed in the laboratory at the Theosophical Society. The others, in the laboratory of the bed, suffered from an inaccuracy of observation, since the reagents that underwent the excitation, that is she and Paul, were themselves the observers who recorded the data. She did notice that the process was occasionally painful, and that Paul seemed more intent on it than she was. She told herself, *This is all a part of what makes the universe work.* Before, when she had observed all those crowds of people filling the pavements and sidewalks and crammed into the houses of cities, it never occurred to her to wonder where they came from, or why their numbers increased slightly but incrementally each year. Now she knew this fact, along with the reason why Stockhausen concentrate caused an electroscope to discharge; and it was Paul who had taught her.

41

* * *

As the years passed Paul gradually became more celebrated and successful, and more controversial. The University and the Academy of Sciences continued to snub him, but his fame in the world grew. He was frequently invited to lecture in Rome or Berlin, and his papers were published in foreign journals. Claire, only a short while before an unknown student at the Sorbonne, now worked at his side as his collaborator.

When her daughter was born she took only two weeks' leave from the laboratory and was soon back at her post at the workbench. She was too thin and impatient to nurse the child, and it was turned over to Mme Lacrosse, the concierge of the house in Rue François-Villon, who had raised several children of her own and was thoroughly competent in the matter. Hermine as an infant seemed to resemble her father in her stiff black hair and her liquid eyes, and her mother in the plain boniness of her features. She was thin and never seemed to gain much weight on the milk which Mme Lacrosse gave her from the bottle. "Oh là now, how pretty she is!" cried Mme Lacrosse. She called in the neighbors to see. They thought it would have been better if Claire stayed home to nurse the child.

In the laboratory at the Theosophical Society, a gloomy room with iron beams in the ceiling and dusty windows looking out onto the courtyard at the rear, Claire was working on the final refinement of the S-metal samples before they were turned over to Delvaux for spectroscopic examination. Her equipment was the fractional crystallization apparatus and the centrifuge, which between them reduced the concentrate until a wagonload of ore became a speck of salt in the bottom of the centrifuge tube. She spent many hours sitting by the centrifuge which spun with a penetrating hum. Occasionally she removed the sample to test its potency with the calibrated electroscope which Paul had designed, handling the tube with her fingers because she dropped it too frequently with the tongs. The centrifuge became her whole life; she immersed her identity in it and its humming became the very pulse of her life-blood, the vibration of corpuscles in her veins. She seldom left the apparatus even to eat; Bloch or one of the assistants would bring her a sandwich at the worktable.

She and Paul had succeeded in reducing a ton of raw Stockhausen earth to less than a milligram of refined concentrate. They found out by accident, coming into the laboratory late one night when the lights were turned out, that the chloride of S-metal was slightly phosphorescent, giving off a blue-green glow that struck the glass vial with pinpoints of violet. More weeks of work on this new discovery followed. When they refined the samples even further they discovered bizarre qualities. The dull white powder, which resembled kitchen salt, tinged its glass receivers mauve and violet in only a few days. A paper wrapped around the glass soon became rotten and decayed into powder. By this time the samples produced enough light to read a newspaper in the dark. The salts of S-metal could also make other materials phosphorescent including the rotor of the centrifuge, the tongs with which they were handled, and even the fingernails of the laboratory workers. The bluff Bloch, who was fond of jokes, commented that Monsieur would always be able to find Madame in the dark. This secondary phosphorescence, however, soon faded, and the burns that the samples left on their fingers were small and evidently harmless. Even the gas given off by the concentrate, confined in narrow tubes, left a reddish inflammation on the skin if carried in the clothing for a few days. A curious fact was that these burns caused no pain at all; the emanations from the concentration seemed to have an analgesic effect.

The time came when they sat down together to write the major paper announcing these discoveries, a monograph that was sure to be controversial, to increase Paul's fame among the general public and to annoy the Sorbonne even more. They had returned to the laboratory after dinner, leaving Hermine with Mme Lacrosse; they had decided to write the paper at night rather than disrupt the routine of the laboratory in the daytime. Claire assembled their notes, and Paul laid out a piece of yellow lined paper and a pen on the worktable. She waited for him to start. Instead he looked at her strangely, with a little smile. He got up and went to the thin glass vial connected to the gas-exhausting apparatus, removed it with his fingers, and brought it to the worktable. It was a piece of ordinary tubing, the diameter of a clinical thermometer, plugged at the ends and filled with a white powder. He fixed it in a clamp over the yellow paper on the worktable. Then he went to the switch on the wall and turned off the electric lights. As their eyes adjusted to the darkness the paper, the pen, and Claire's notes were dimly illuminated with the spectral blue-green glow from the vial. Paul took up the pen and began writing.

The investigations conducted by the joint signatories have led to the discovery of a new element, with qualities hitherto unknown in any form of matter. It was in this paper too that the name of the new element appeared for the first time, a word so simple and natural that afterward they could never remember which of them had invented it, so that it seemed that they had always known it: glowstone.

With the publication of this monograph a great deal of public attention was focused on the work of the laboratory, and events followed with an astonishing rapidity. In 1902 the Savarin Institute for Research in the Transmutation of Matter was founded with funds from the Ministry of Mines and private donations; the Sorbonne remained aloof. The title of the Institute, in fact, was considered a direct slap in the face at the University, reviving as it did the terminology of medieval alchemy that was anathema to the professors. The laboratory was moved to new quarters at 5 Rue de l'École-de-Médecine, in an unused medical theater with connecting rooms for offices and workshops. A larger staff was appointed, including Paul Lancelot, a physicist from Grenoble who was assigned the task of finding practical uses for the new element in industry and medicine while the others continued their research in pure science. Bloch, who was in his sixties by this time and suffered from rheumatism, retired and was replaced by a young workman named Onyx Fabre. A brass plaque was put up beside the street gate with the name of the new institute. The success of glowstone in treating certain diseases brought widespread publicity to the work of the Savarins. More invitations came from foreign universities and governments; Paul was honored in Stockholm, Rome, and Madrid, and Clarie and Paul went with Hermine to London, where Paul received the Gold Medal of the Royal Academy.

In London Paul made a speech of acceptance at the Royal Academy which astonished everyone, even Claire herself. The thin physicist who was so shy and reserved with individuals, or in a small group, rose to an unexpected eloquence before the audience of distinguished scientists and patrons in the banquet hall. Describing his work of many years, first alone and then with his wife at his side, he spoke modestly but with evident emotion. He held out to the listeners his burn-scarred hands, and then reached into his vest pocket and took out a small vial of refined glowstone salts, the same sample, in fact, that he and Claire had used for the illumination in which they wrote their monograph. An usher came up with an electroscope, and he demonstrated how the mere proximity of the vial caused the vanes of gold leaf to fall, indicating the impressive power of the emanations.

He turned the tiny tube of glass in his fingers. "In this small vial is enclosed the most extraordinary substance to come to the knowledge of mankind since the discovery of the lodestone by the ancient Phoenicians. It is the elixir of the twentieth century, a fresh hope for mankind in its struggle against disease and darkness. The emanations from glowstone have already been proved useful in the treatment of cancers, abscesses, and the abnormal growth of certain glands. It also undoubtedly has a curative effect on arthritis and on Dupuytren's contracture, a painful disease of the hands. Some medical investigators believe that tiny grains of the element, implanted in the lungs of tuberculosis patients, might kill the bacilli that cause the disease."

He went on for more than an hour in his low sibilant voice, speaking English with difficulty but with precision. Toward the end he asked for the lights in the room to be dimmed so that he could show the audience the phosphorescence in the vial.

The blue-green glow was clearly visible in the tube of glass in his fingers. "This," he told them in a hushed and steady voice, "is the light of the new century. Painted on watch faces and compasses, glowstone makes them visible in the dark. In time, as the process is improved and the pure metallic element is produced, it may be used for public lighting, replacing the electric bulbs of Mr. Edison. Its uses in warfare and in medicine are also unlimited. I am well aware—all of my collaborators are—that glowstone in the hands of a criminal or deranged person might be a menace to mankind. The same is true of the dynamite invented by Mr. Nobel, which is useful to miners but dangerous in the hands of terrorists. Such risks are always attendant upon new discoveries in science, from gunpowder to vaccination. Used with care and intelligence, glowstone may well prove to be the greatest boon to mankind since the invention of fire."

At the end he asked Claire too to rise. "Ladies and gentlemen," he told them in a voice at a higher pitch, trembling a little with emotion, "my wife and I stand before you tonight as simple workers in science. The work that any one of us can do, the contribution that we can make to the welfare of man, is slight. It is not the individual but science itself that we must respect and venerate. We must stand humble before its profundity, and we must use what it offers us with care, with wisdom, and with genuine humanity, for the benefit of all men. This small glass tube that I offer you is more important than any of us. It has the power, perhaps—we do not yet know everything about it, although we know much—to bring light and life to suffering mankind, to alleviate pain, to broaden the scope of our understanding of the very nature of matter and the mysterious energy it contains. Let us go forward hand in hand to be sure this gift is used for the good of all humanity." His voice fell almost to a whisper. "Vive la France. Vive l'Angleterre. Et vive la Science."

There was a moment of silence, then a ripple of applause which quick grew to a roar, filling the hall and lasting for some time. It ended only when Paul left the podium to press the many waiting hands that stretched out to greet him.

GLOWSTONE

The next day Paul carried the small vial of glowstone salts back to Paris in his vest pocket, since he didn't want to entrust it to his baggage. As they undressed in the bedroom in Rue François-Villon that night, he found a small reddened patch on his skin at the point where he had carried the vial. Showing Claire this and the scars on his hands, he told her in a whimsical voice, "My Stigmata." The burn from the vial was at exactly the point where Christ had been pierced by a Roman spear in his side.

Even after these honors fell upon them, Paul and Claire had little life except for their work together in the laboratory. They seldom went out in the evening and never went on a holiday, except for an occasional summer excursion on a Sunday to Bougival where they had spent their brief honeymoon. There they would walk along the quay leading small Hermine by the hand, gazing at the artists painting the picturesque curve of the Seine and the island just opposite the inn where they had stayed, and nodding politely to the other strollers, working-class people with their children for the most part. As the afternoon ended they would sit down in a café while Hermine happily ate an ice-cream or a pastry. She had a sensuality in her character lacking in either Claire or Paul, and when she was a little girl it took the form of a delight in sweets and desserts, the sensuality of children. Her favorite was an éclair, or even better a mille-feuille, its "thousand leaves" of fragile pastry layered with crème Chantilly and vanilla. Once a waiter suggested, "And for you, ma petite. Perhaps a savarin?"

"A savarin?"

Claire and Paul were dubious; it did contain alcohol. They were silent, and when it came Hermine consumed it to the last crumb, getting the final drops of liqueur with a spoon. It was one of the most delightful discoveries of her childhood that the word of her last name was also something good to eat, a cake soaked with rum and kirsch.

Paul himself would take a cup of tea, and Claire only a glass of ice water with a slice of lemon in it. They would return to

Paris for dinner; they almost never went to a restaurant except to the modest Bouillon Duval where the three of them could dine for five francs.

On these Sunday outings they never explained to Hermine the reason why Bougival had a special meaning in their lives.

"And there is the inn," Paul would always remind Claire, as they sat at the café table only a short distance from it.

"Yes," she would reply, pressing her lips together.

They never explained the meaning of this ritual exchange to Hermine, and she never had the wit to inquire. It was only years later that she came upon the receipted bill from the inn with the date, and putting it together with their marriage certificate pieced together the facts. The reason that Paul had chosen Bougival for their honeymoon, as a matter of fact, was not for its beauty or the picturesque river scenery, but because he had gone there years before on an outing with school friends and it was the only place on the Seine that he knew how to get to, taking the train from St.-Lazare to Chatou and from there an omnibus that ran only in the summer.

On Sundays when they didn't go to Bougival, they would often go for a stroll in the Luxembourg Gardens, which were only five minutes' walk from the Institute in Rue de l'École-de-Médecine. Usually Paul and Claire would look in at the laboratory, where someone was sure to be working even on Sunday, Onyx Fabre or the Swiss assistant Délicienne Maedl. Then they would go off to the Luxembourg, by way of Rue Monsieur-le-Prince and past the gloomy statue of the lovers Acis and Galatea being spied on by the giant Polyphemus, which always gave Hermine a little frisson. This was the total extent of their amusements.

Until her father died, when she was sixteen, Hermine had never been to a café in Paris, and never attended a concert, a recital, or an exhibition of art. Her knowledge of music was confined to the brass bands that played on Sunday afternoons in the Luxembourg, and of art to her occasional glimpses of the painters' canvases at Bougival. Her parents never stopped to look at the paintings, nor did they linger very long by the brass bands in the gardens. Her mother on Sundays wore the same black serge dress in which she was married, winter and summer. In the winter she added a black velvet paletot and a scarf over her hat, and in the summer she perspired, a thin, acrid, and curiously inoffensive odor that Hermine could recall years later as though it were still in her nostrils. She always carried the same bag, black tapestry with pastel figures and a clasp at the top in gray gunmetal. Her father too wore black, with an old homburg stained green around the band in winter and an equally ancient panama in the summer. Meeting someone in the gardens, perhaps Professor Puisson-Lepuy, the only member of the Sorbonne faculty he was on speaking terms with, Paul would raise his hat absentmindedly.

"Bonjour, Professeur."

"Bonjour, Docteur."

"Fine weather we're having."

"Very fine for winter, Docteur."

"And that is your little girl?"

"Yes, that's our Hermine."

"Well, au revoir, Docteur."

"Au revoir, Professeur."

During this exchange Claire would say not a word, still held back by the awe of professors that she had felt as a young girl straight from Brussels. Sometimes they would meet one of Paul's former colleagues from the School of Mines, and he would lift his hat without speaking. Even though they were honored in London, Stockholm, and Rome and their work was described in magazines in America, they had no friends in Paris except for Lancelot and the others in the laboratory, especially the faithful Fabre. Later, when Hermine made friends at school, she never brought them home. Such an encounter, of the outer world with the secret and confined life of the family in Rue François-Villon, would have been unthinkable to her.

The thing that seemed strange to her, as she observed the families of her friends at school and found out how others lived, was that her mother never bought a new dress. When she referred to the black serge she called it simply "my dress." In the laboratory, where she spent most of her waking hours, she wore a shapeless gray skirt and blouse with a stained laboratory smock over them. With this went black stockings and sturdy workman's shoes, since the floor of the laboratory was often contaminated with acid or other dangerous substances. The black dress hung in the wardrobe in the apartment six days out of seven.

Hermine discovered only years later that this black dress with the embroidered military collar was not always the same one; when it wore out, every five years or so, Claire bought another one exactly like it. It was, in fact, a kind of uniform for an order of lay Sisters who did charity work in the poorer quarters of the city, and was kept in stock by the Bon Marché in all sizes. It suited her needs exactly; it was made of good material and the workmanship was excellent. The Bon Marché was a store that could be counted on for quality. The choice of color was a prudent one; black went with everything and was suitable for all occasions, from a Sunday walk in the gardens to the presentation of the Gold Medal at the Royal Academy in London. Although she hadn't anticipated it, the dress served as well for the burial of her husband in the Cimetière Montparnasse.

After Paul's death Claire took over the directorship of the Institute, with the double task now of continuing the research she and Paul had been doing and supervising the work of the others. To everyone's surprise, she proved to be a more efficient and more demanding administrator than Paul himself had been. "Madame wishes" became the formula that decided every question in the work of the laboratory, down to the last detail. Occasionally the others permitted themselves witticisms on this subject, telling each other, "Madame wishes you to change your socks more often," or "Madame wishes you not to chew with your mouth open." But not Fabre, and not Lancelot; the others were careful to keep their ironies from these two faithful ones. Her grief was evident to everyone; she never smiled and she permitted herself even less diversion than she had when Paul was alive. The Sunday walks in the Luxembourg ended. Yet at times she seemed almost to forget her dead husband and to throw herself into the work of the Institute as though Paul had never existed, as though it were something that she herself had conceived and brought into being. She imposed on the Institute a distinct personal flair, a thing it had never had when Paul was director. The Institute became a projection of her own personality: austere, hardworking, devoted, and humorless, filled with a solemn, almost religious sense of the importance of glowstone and the work being done in the laboratory. In the mornings she devoted herself to administrative matters, and in the afternoons she worked with Delvaux on the precise determination of the atomic weight of glowstone and its place in the table of elements. In the evenings, still at the Institute, she worked on the scientific papers which she published now in her own name. She seldom came home to the apartment before eleven, and in the morning she was gone before Hermine got up to fix her own breakfast and leave for school. Even on Sundays she often went back to the laboratory to work, while Hermine visited friends or worked on her lessons in the apartment.

Although Claire knew me well, she never suspected in those days that I was observing her every act and gesture in order to fit them together, much later, into the connected story that lies hidden in everyone's life. And I myself was unaware of this; it was only later that I came to grasp my role in her life as the teller of her story. From my privileged position, as inconspicuous and as attentive as the proverbial fly on the wall, I watched as the drama of her life was played out act by act. The ordinary routine of things, in those times of 1906 and the following years, brought us together almost every day, but I never knew her intimately. I doubt if anyone did; perhaps Paul did at one time, but he was passed away now. Her story therefore has to be pieced together, half guessed at, and filled in by the imagination. I was present at the burial in the Cimetière Montparnasse, but I couldn't guess at the impulse that led to her strange gesture of throwing dirt from the grave over the other mourners, and to this day I can only conjecture about it. She lived a private life, inaccessible even to those closest to her, her daughter, her co-worker Paul Lancelot, and the faithful mechanic Fabre.

An incident involving Fabre, about a year after her husband's death, may throw some light on her state of mind, or her spiritual state, in those times when she was still suffering constantly from grief at the loss of Paul. It was told to me by another worker in the laboratory; but it wasn't Fabre and it wasn't Lancelot.

Onyx Fabre, a native of Marseille, was not specially trained in science and in fact not very well educated. He attended school in Marseille until he was sixteen and then came to Paris as a bicycle mechanic. He was skilled with his hands and clever with anything mechanical; there were few broken clocks, household appliances, or children's toys that he couldn't mend quickly. The new science of electricity he mastered instantly. He even invented an apparatus for cleaning carpets, in which a boy worked the treadles of a vacuum pump while a housemaid applied a long flexible tube to the carpet, but it didn't catch on.

Fabre had come to the laboratory at the Theosophical Society once, before the Institute was founded, to repair Delvaux's spectroscope; he grasped the principle of the apparatus instantly and fabricated a new brass grating holder to replace the wooden one that was constantly going out of line. When the Institute was founded a short time later Paul engaged him as a handyman and general mechanic, but he soon showed himself to be far more. Even though he had no theoretical grasp of science, he quickly saw the point of the work going on in the laboratory. It was only a few months until he could be trusted to do his part of the scientific work along with the others. In addition to Lancelot, Delvaux, and Épinasse, there were a half-dozen assistants in the laboratory at this time, most of them graduates of the Sorbonne, and at first there was a certain amount of resentment at Fabre's position almost as their equal. But he soon disarmed them with his evident honesty, his keen grasp of any mechanical problem and his quickness in solving it, his untiring good humor, and his charm.

At this time he was a man of thirty with a broad face, stubby fingers, and a typical Provençal expression, good-natured and open, with large dark eyes and a mouth quick to smile. His fingers, like everyone else's in the laboratory, were scarred with burns from the active refined ore. He earned good wages, and his ambition was to save enough to open a bicycle shop in Marseille, catering particularly to racing bicyclists. His business sense was excellent and it seemed likely that he would make a success of this venture. In the meantime he was an indispensable member of the laboratory staff.

One day in the late spring, about a year after Paul's death, he came by the Institute to say goodbye before leaving on a holiday. He brought with him another Southerner named Louis Carbon. The two of them planned to tour the Cévennes for two weeks on their bicycles, which they wheeled into the laboratory to show the others. They were well-built touring machines, imported from England and fitted with acetylene lamps, luggage carriers, and the latest model of rim-clamp brakes. The luggage, a pair of saddlebags for each, was mounted over the rear wheels. Fabre proudly showed them his photographic apparatus, promising to bring them back pictures of the tour. It was the latest model of camera made in America by the Eastman Company, with a leather bellows so it could be folded up and carried in the pocket. Instead of packets the film was a new kind that came on spools, and he showed them these too. Fabre was excessively proud of this camera and referred to "my Kodak" several times during the half hour he was in the laboratory. Then he and Carbon departed; they would ride their bicycles across Paris to the Gare de Lyon and from there take a train to the South. Everyone shook hands and Claire reminded Fabre not to have an accident. In her own mind she wondered why anyone would want to take a holiday. It suggested to her that Fabre wasn't entirely happy with his work at the Institute; if he was, why would he want to leave it even for a few days? She pondered over this mystery for some time, but didn't succeed in grasping why someone would prefer riding a bicycle to working in a laboratory.

Fabre came back to the laboratory as promised after the two-week holiday. He had not had an accident in the Cévennes. But when he appeared on that Monday morning he wasn't entirely the old Fabre, and he didn't immediately set to work in the laboratory as he usually did. Instead he had his camera with him and something else in an envelope.

"Look at this, Madame. See what has happened to my film."

He produced the negatives from the envelope. The long strips of celluloid were black as ink from one end to the other. If they had been printed the pictures would have been totally white, as though the camera had been pointed at the sun. But the camera had not been pointed at the sun. Even the ends of the negatives, which were not exposed when the lens was opened, were black as jet. In some way the film had been exposed while it was enclosed in total darkness inside the camera. A glare of invisible light, of occult light, had penetrated the camera and the lightproof wrapping of the film.

"You must have exposed the film when you loaded it into the camera."

"Impossible, Madame." Fabre got out the Kodak and showed how it was loaded. Only the end was unwound from the spool, and the film was backed with a thick sheet of opaque black paper.

"Then there must be a defect in the camera. It isn't properly lightproof.

"Impossible again. If there had been a leak in the camera it would have exposed the film only in places."

"Perhaps the film itself was defective."

"It came from America, still wrapped in the lead foil in which it was packed."

By this time most of the staff of the laboratory had gathered around to listen: Delvaux, Épinasse, the two assistants Carlo Bini and Délicienne Maedl, and several others. There was a silence after Fabre's remarks. Everyone in the room knew that Fabre had brought the loaded camera and the extra film into the laboratory to show them before he left on his trip. And they knew also that Madame wasn't being candid, that she was concealing something they all knew, except for Fabre who had no scientific training.

Finally it was Délicienne Maedl who spoke. In spite of her

54

inviting name the young Swiss woman was plain as a post, with an angular figure and a craggy face. She wore her hair like a partly opened tent out of which she peered with her soft Alpine eyes, the eyes of a chamois. But she was an excellent chemist.

"Madame, the emanations that come from the glowstone samples." They were standing in the center of the laboratory where the final refinement of the active salts was carried out. "Isn't it possible that they might be damaging to photographic film?"

"It's well known that glowstone emanations affect photographic film. In fact this is one way of detecting their presence. I'm surprised that you don't know this, Mademoiselle."

But of course she did know it. They were all startled by this new deviousness of Madame, by this slight edge of malice in her voice. Fabre looked at her perplexed.

"But Madame. When I came here with the camera I never went near the apparatus. I only stood over there at the side by the door. I was several meters away from any source of refined glowstone."

"You'd better not bring your camera to the laboratory," she said shortly. "I'll pay you for the film if you like."

"But the camera is designed to exclude all forms of light. It's made partly of aluminum. It's impossible that the emanations could penetrate it."

"The glowstone here in the laboratory is highly refined. We're now working with the pure chloride. Someday soon we shall produce the element itself. In high concentration, glowstone emanations can pass through metal."

"Then they penetrate our bodies too?"

"Very likely."

Dèlicienne and Bini exchanged a glance. It was more than likely, it was an established fact.

"Do you mean, Madame," said Fabre, "that as I'm standing here now these waves are passing through my body? Isn't that perhaps harmful to the health? Because, at closer range, the emanations burn the skin." He raised his hand to show his scarred fingertips.

"See here, my dear Onyx." Madame seemed out of sorts.

"We're discussing things we all know. If you don't want to work in the laboratory, don't do so. In any case don't bring your camera into it. The emanations from glowstone pass through the body as they do through everything else. As for whether they are damaging to the health, it's just the opposite. They're useful in treating cancers and ulcers, they are used in the enlargement of lymphatic glands, and they can dry up ringworm. It's very likely that in time they'll be used to treat tuberculosis."

He still appeared dubious and troubled.

"Imagine this, Onyx. Suppose you're a soldier and you receive a bullet wound. The doctors are unable to find the bullet. But imagine that we have you lie on a table with a piece of photographic film enclosed in black paper under you and a small particle of glowstone above you. When the film is developed, the shadow of the bullet will show on it, because the emanations can't penetrate lead, not at least until they're very powerful. Then, knowing exactly where he bullet is, the surgeon can operate to remove it."

"And this causes no harm to the soldier?"

"Of course not."

"But I'm not a soldier. Here in the laboratory we—"

She interrupted him. "Then how can you say that glowstone is damaging to the health?"

Lancelot took her by the arm and led her away from the others. When he saw that they were still watching he said, "Go away. Go on back to your work. We've wasted far too much time this morning." They turned and drifted slowly away to their work places, Délicienne looking back once.

"Claire, you're overwrought. You must compose yourself. You're perfectly right in everything you say. The important thing is that these personal matters mustn't be allowed to interfere with the work of the laboratory."

He was still gently holding her arm. Mechanically she raised her hand to push him away.

"I'm perfectly composed," she told him. As a matter of fact she wasn't perfectly composed. She was far from anger; she was incapable, she believed, of anger or personal resentment.

GLOWSTONE

What she felt was something else. In the moment when she confronted Fabre over the camera something stirred in her, something primordial and warm. She had found herself speaking with emotion to a man, a thing she hadn't done in the year since Paul's death. She had thought that the pain lessened a little with the passing months but it came back to her in a flood of inner tremoring. She murmured, "Paul, Paul"; to herself, she hoped, but Lancelot heard it. At first he imagined she was speaking to him, then he realized his mistake.

The dead are always with us, Claire thought. We may think we have relegated them into the forgetfulness which is for us a cessation of pain, but they have a way of stealing through the dark and coming back to us, sometimes when we least expect it. They exist, not in their atoms which have been dispersed through the indifferent universe, but in the invisible labyrinths of our minds, where there are realms far larger than the mythical Elysian Fields for them to inhabit, lands whose existence we don't even suspect. When they return, they may trouble our dreams, or lie just under the surface of our waking thoughts, to be brought to life abruptly, with the vividness of a vision, by a glimpse of a street corner or a park, an elusive odor, a chance word spoken by another. The dead are not responsible for their actions, but we are responsible to them and we must answer to them. It's no good for us to remind them, and ourselves, that they no longer exist, that the superstitions of religion have long been banished, that the matter that composed them has long since been absorbed in other matter and reborn in new forms. The dead lurk and wait their moment to show themselves, although sometimes in disguise, and sometimes in ways we are hardly aware of until we examine the strange life of the unconscious.

About this time she began to be troubled by a recurring dream. It was always much the same but varied in its details. She was wandering in an unknown city, something like Brussels or Paris but not exactly like either. The buildings of the city were modern, made of stone or concrete. At the same time they had the qualities of classical temples or archaeological ruins; the edges which appeared sharp from a distance were actually crumbling and soft when viewed from a closer range. However she was seldom able to approach them very closely; instead she found herself going endlessly down the streets looking for something and sensing that she had somehow lost her way. As is often the case in dreams, she had the feeling that she was not properly clad for the occasion—but what occasion was it?—or even that part of her body was indecently exposed.

Perhaps she was alone, and perhaps she had another person with her, a person smaller than her, depending on her, and she must guide this other person and protect her along the way they were going. But this other person frequently strayed from her sight, and possibly didn't exist. This caused her anxiety, because even if this other person didn't exist she was still responsible for her. She wondered whether she ought to set aside her quest, perhaps, and go and look for her in the streets she had already passed.

And what was this quest? She wasn't quite sure. Or rather, in dreams it isn't necessary for a quest to have a meaning, we simply feel that we are questing and must keep on until we find something, we aren't sure what. In any case she had a sense of the general direction she ought to go. In a part of her mind she was aware of her goal not far away from her, in the way we may glimpse the Eiffel Tower or the twin steeples of the Notre-Dame over the rooftops without being sure which of the curving streets we ought to take to reach it. But these weren't real streets, or they didn't behave like real streets. Their main qualities were their unreason and their inevitability. As she followed the street she was on, it might cross the others at odd angles and often went over them on bridges or under them in tunnels. There were at least three levels in the city, and it wasn't likely that the level of any one street she was on would be the same as the level of the place she was trying to get to. Often she could see another street that she wanted to reach in order to continue her search, but the street she was on led over it and away in another direction, or curved around so gradually that it was some time before she realized that she was walking away from her mysterious goal and not towards it. (Come, she told the person she was holding by the hand, we must hurry because time is slipping away and if nightfall comes we won't be able to find it.)

Wandering among the rectilinear buildings, she sometimes caught sight of a temple in the classical manner toward which all the streets of the city seemed to lead, but the streets curved away from it or slanted in another direction and she lost sight of it again. In this city of her dream it was always daylight, although the atmosphere was gray and insubstantial and there were no shadows. She was never tired and she didn't feel anxious or afraid; she only felt a sense of guilt that she hadn't succeeded in finding what she was trying to find, which might be something as simple as the hotel where she was staying, or the railroad station from which she was to leave for another city. Perhaps it was the white temple, but she often forgot the temple and was reminded of it only when she caught sight of it over the rooftops again. She was curious about the temple and longed to reach it so that she could see what was inside it, but at the same time she was afraid of what she might find, perhaps a scene of horrible sacrifice or some obscenity out of an old pagan culture. She didn't know how such a thing could be allowed, but the authorities were not aware of it, probably, or perhaps they allowed it in the way that mosques are sometimes allowed in a modern city like Paris. When she came closer to the temple she saw that there was a light in its interior, visible now and then between its columns or through its marble porticos. She found some steps leading from her street down to the next level, where there was a street leading toward the temple. She followed it, and noticed that it was night now, although it had always been daylight in the city before. There were no streetlamps and no lights in the windows of the shops, nothing but the gray shapes of the buildings. She stole along the street toward the faint light that came from the door of the temple just around the corner.

When she turned the corner she was no longer aware of the greenish light, or rather now it seemed to be coming from behind her. In the deserted street something was lying on the pavement. It was a small shadow like a rag or an abandoned garment. When she came closer she saw it was a dead dog. Unable to move herself, she screamed at the person with her to run, but her scream died in her throat and she couldn't make a sound. At that moment she woke up.

She was covered with perspiration and trembling all over. It was some time before she recovered her composure. She got up to fetch a glass of water in the kitchen. Across the passage and through the open door she saw Hermine lying asleep in her room, a tuft of dark hair showing against the pillow and her small neat rear thrust up in the blankets. It was only Hermine, she told herself. It was when I went with Hermine to Brussels to visit her grandparents and we couldn't find the railway station.

III

"Let me help you carry that thing, Claire."

"I can handle it perfectly well."

"Then let a porter take it."

"A porter! Certainly not."

"I can carry it for a little while, Maman," said Hermine.

"You're too much of a scatterbrain."

They were picking their way through the crowd in the Gare de l'Est. The thing she was carrying was a leaden case weighing fifteen pounds, and inside it a particle of metal the size of a match head, in a glass tube with the air exhausted and sealed with wax. By this time Claire, with the help of the others in the laboratory, had succeeded in isolating glowstone in its pure metallic form. No one knew what pure glowstone looked like and no one ever would. Presumably it was a dull silver metal, but in its pure form it was so strongly luminescent that the eye saw only a source of blue-green light; the metal itself couldn't be seen any more than you could see the filament of an incandescent bulb when it was lighted. If she had possessed a gram of it—but she didn't have a gram—it would have represented the refined product of seventy tons of ore. Its monetary value could be calculated only by the labor needed to extract it, millions of francs. The heavy lead case was necessary because of the strength of its emanations, far more powerful than those of the chloride salt.

The three of them—Claire, Lancelot, and Hermine—were leaving on a lecture tour which was to take Claire to Strasbourg, Utrecht, and Oxford and then on to America. In October, after the lecture in England, Lancelot would go back to Paris to carry on the work of the laboratory, where he served as deputy director in Claire's absence. Hermine too would have to leave her then; she had finished the lycée now and was beginning her studies at the University, where the term began at the end of the month. Claire would go on to America by herself, for lectures in Princeton, Philadelphia, and Denver.

Claire didn't enjoy the idea of speaking before large bodies, but it was a thing that Paul had done, and she was resolved to do her duty in this respect as she did in other things. In Strasbourg she gave an illustrated lecture on the discovery of glowstone and on the work of the Institute. She repeated Paul's trick of demonstrating the power of glowstone with an electroscope, removing the sample from the lead case and holding it carefully with the tongs. But now she did it before a magic lantern which projected it enormously magnified onto a screen. When the gold leaves fell inside the glass bell there was a burst of applause, even though it was a simple demonstration that any schoolteacher could do. She gave the identical lecture at Utrecht and then at Oxford, where Hermine disgraced herself by failing to attend the lecture in the afternoon and instead going punting on the Isis with students.

When they met again at the hotel she told her, "You might have learned something from the lecture, you know, even though you've heard it several times."

"Oh, I did hear a lecture, on my charms."

"And who was the lecturer?"

"It was a trio, one in my punt and two in another, so it was perfectly innocent."

Claire didn't know what to think. It was a curious notion, that the more suitors you had the more innocent it was. "You're too young to have admirers, you know."

"I'm the same age as you were when you first came to Paris."

"I didn't have admirers. I had your father."

"Oh, Maman. They're just boys. I'm perfectly capable of taking care of myself."

When Claire told all this to Lancelot he hesitated for a moment, then he said, "I wonder if you realize, Claire, that your daughter is no longer a child."

"Of course I do. What are you saying? That she should be allowed to go punting with students or that she should not?"

"All I'm saying is that you imagine your daughter is always the same person, but a woman isn't the same person as a child. One has to be more vigilant with a daughter after she's reached a certain age, and on the other hand one has to allow her more freedom. If Hermine . . ."

"Oh good heavens, Lancelot, you're talking nonsense. Stop and listen to yourself. Should I be more vigilant or should I allow her more freedom? And what business is it of yours anyhow?" she said sharply, forgetting that she herself had told the whole thing to him in the hope of getting his advice. Lancelot was a fool, even though he was a brilliant scientist, and it was a mistake to confide in him. After all, what Hermine had done was perfectly normal. It was very different from what she herself would have done, but she had enough insight to recognize that she wasn't the same as other people. The other girls, at the Académie Ferney where she had gone as a girl, thought of nothing but boys. Still it was all very strange to her, how Hermine was born, sent to school, given deportment lessons and Italian, acquired a polka-dot blouse, let her hair grow and decided to cut it after all, and learned to smile in that artful way, all in the space of the few moments that had elapsed since she and Paul had settled down to housekeeping in Rue François-Villon. She examined herself in the pier glass in the hall of the hotel; she was just the same, it was the others who changed, put on gray wigs to impersonate themselves as old men or women, or changed overnight from children to young girls who went punting with boys. On the whole, to people she preferred glowstone, which was mysterious but more predictable, not subject to whims or fantasies or vapors of the head. It changed too, but only very slowly, so that after a thousand years, according to calculations that she and Lancelot had made, there was still half of its original substance left.

Both Hermine and Lancelot were uneasy about the thought of Claire going on to America alone. Perhaps, Lancelot suggested, someone else from the Institute could accompany her, to deal with porters and help her with the baggage, the faithful Onyx Fabre, of Délicienne Maedl—she would be ideal—a strong young Swiss woman who had milked cows as a girl and had muscles like billiard balls. But she rejected the suggestion.

"My dears, I'm quite capable of going to America or anywhere else by myself. I used to travel a great deal with Paul and I know how it's done. Besides I'm being met everywhere by the people sponsoring my lectures. So don't worry about me."

"Worrying, Claire, is not a voluntary activity."

"Well then, worry all you like, but I'm going anyhow. Onyx and Délicienne can't be spared, and it's my duty to go. A good deal of the philanthropy that supports the Institute," she reminded them, "comes from America."

She had to carry the heavy lead case by herself; everything else could be managed by porters. She said goodbye to them at Victoria Station—they would return to Paris by train and Channel steamer—and the next day sailed from Southhampton on the *Majestic,* a crack liner which would make the crossing in five days. She was a little ashamed of having spent so much on the ticket, even though the trip was paid for by a grant from the French Ministry of Culture, and she allowed herself only a second-class cabin. On shipboard she had nothing to do with the other passengers and spent her time assembling notes for a paper on hypotheses on the gradual loss of weight of glowstone as it gave off its emanations.

In New York she was met by a delegation consisting of the

GLOWSTONE

French Consul and a committee of professors, who took her directly to her lecture at Princeton. Even though she felt she wasn't a very effective public speaker, she charmed her audience completely with her competence, her modesty, and the obvious note of emotion with which she spoke of her years of work at the side of Paul.

"My husband was a saint of science," she told them. "I cannot claim to be that. I was only a helpmeet, and he is my constant companion in thought today as I continue in the task which he first conceived, and which he carried out almost to the sight of his goal. Glowstone is a monument to his memory, and in this case"—she pointed to the leaden box before her— "I carry his soul as we scientists understand the soul. The light I have shown you a few moments ago in this darkened room is the light of the future, of the new century. May it help to dispel a little the darkness of ignorance and suffering that has lain over mankind from the beginning of its history." The words were Paul's, only slightly adapted to fit the new audience and the new circumstances. When she ended they were followed by the same applause that had greeted Paul's address in London years before.

From Princeton it was only a short distance to Philadelphia, where she was to give her lecture at the University of Pennsylvania. At the station she looked around for a delegation like the one that had met her in New York, but there was no one on the platform but a young man in a tweed suit and a flat workman's cap, who stood smiling at her from a little distance away. Presently he strolled up to her and said, "Hullo, you must be Madame Savarin-Decker. Let me take that case from you. Where's the rest of your baggage?"

He told her his name; he was a professor of physics at the university and he had been "told off," as he said, to take care of her during her visit. It was certainly very different from her reception by the solemn trio of professors in New York. The young physicist was tall and half-bald, grave and at the same time smiling. He treated her in a courteous but offhand way, a casualness so genuine that she hardly knew whether to be offended or not. He put his hands in his pockets when he had nothing else to do with them, a thing you never did in the presence of a lady in Europe.

She went to her hotel to freshen up for an hour or so, then, since it was still more than an hour before her lecture, the young physicist (she could never remember his name, it was something German that began with an H) insisted on taking her to see his own laboratory, which was on the campus not far from the lecture hall. The first thing she saw in it was a bicycle; he told her he rode it to the laboratory every day from his apartment in the suburbs. With the playful smile he seemed to wear at all times, he showed her his cycling cap and the metal clips to fit over his trouser legs. He seemed more like Onyx Fabre than like a real scientist; and with this thought she felt a sudden pang of homesickness for her laboratory in Rue de l'École-de-Médecine, with its familiar acrid smells, its humming centrifuge, and the worn worktable covered with acid stains and burns.

In his own laboratory—which he was attempting to show her, although he had some difficulty getting her attention—he was doing research that in some ways was parallel to hers. He was working on the X rays recently discovered by Roentgen, which like the emanations from glowstone had the power of penetrating solid matter and affecting a photographic plate on the other side. X rays had already proved useful in detecting foreign objects in the human body, he told her, and were considered more efficient and safer than other forms of radiation. She bristled a little at this implied criticism of her beloved glowstone; she didn't care to listen to his further explanations and cut him off rather shortly. If he noticed this, he said nothing and went on smiling.

Her lecture in the middle of the afternoon was attended by a small group of scientists and students. They were knowledgeable and interested in her work, but seemed unimpressed by the trick of discharging the electroscope in front of the magic lantern. A professor in a linen suit told her in his American twang, "We use that ourselves as a demonstration for our beginning students." It was the second time she had been treated with scant courtesy in the same afternoon. It was a new sensation for her. She became annoyed and cut her lecture short. A handful of people came up to the podium afterward to look at her sample of glowstone, but they seemed reluctant to approach it.

"Of course you wear protective clothing when you work with such materials." It was the professor in the linen suit again, the chairman of the department.

"Protective clothing? I wear my ordinary laboratory smock."

The professor smiled discreetly and exchanged glances with the others. "And how long have you been working with these materials?"

"How long? For more than twenty years. Although it's only recently, of course, that we've had available samples of the pure element."

Still curious but cautious, they watched while she put away the glass tube in its case. The young physicist, who had been one of those exchanging glances, hesitated for a moment and then bravely picked up the case. "You didn't tell me what was in this thing," he said. He accompanied her back to her hotel for another freshening-up, then took her out to dinner at a place called Barney's Center City Steak House. He said, "I thought you might like to see what a real American dinner is like." The meal was one that might have been conceived by a redskin on the prairie: a piece of charred beefsteak, a potato baked with its skin on, and corn on the cob, which she had heard about as a child from her father. When the young physicist demonstrated how it was eaten she recalled that she had seen hogs in Belgium eating corn in exactly the same way. She absolutely refused to emulate him. With his usual smile, as though he was amused by everything but still taking her request perfectly seriously, he cut it off the cob for her with a knife.

Claire's last lecture in America was to be in Denver. This occasion was a little different from the others. She was to give her lecture not in a university but before a civic group that had supported the Savarin Institute over many years, from the time it was founded. The Denver engagement was partly for the purpose of thanking these people and showing them the glowstone their generosity had produced. She had also learned that there were mine tailings in the mountains of Colorado, the so-called Telluride ores, that were almost as rich in active elements as the Stockhausen ores; samples had been sent to the Institute for testing and found to contain appreciable amounts of glowstone. The ore from Transylvania would give out in only a few more years, and she was anxious to assure herself of a reliable supply of this raw material that was essential to her work. She had an appointment in her hotel with a certain Mr. White to discuss the possible purchase of these ores.

This country which was her father's native land seemed stranger and stranger to Claire as the train carried her west. The hills of Pennsylvania and eastern Ohio gave way to bleaker rolling country of cornfields and small factory towns. She paused briefly in Chicago, then the train set off again over prairies which seemed endless. Hour after hour, through the night and on into the next day, it crawled over a vast plain of wheat fields, broken only now and then by a small town with its three or four concrete silos, like dolmens left behind by some prehistoric race of giants. These prairies were fatiguing; after a while she longed for the journey to end.

Then on the second day from Chicago she looked out the window and saw something ahead to the west. Above the horizon gray shapes with streaks of white appeared, clouds perhaps, although they had an extraordinary solidity to them. After another half an hour she grasped what it was: a mountain range so high that it seemed to float in the air over the horizon, an immense wall of granite bringing the prairie at last to an end. She could see snowcapped peaks even though it was only November. At the foot of these mountains was Denver.

Her reception committee at the station consisted of a trio of society women from the association that had sent funds to the Institute. They were waiting in a little row as she got off the train, carrying the leaden case in her hand. She was wearing her black serge dress with her capelike paletot over it; she had never owned an overcoat. Her hat was a drum-shaped affair of black with a veil. The three American women stared at her curiously. They themselves were wearing flowered silk dresses that came to their ankles, white shoes, and broad straw hats. The four of them, along with Claire's baggage, got into two cabs and were driven to the Brown Palace Hotel.

After the committee left her she found herself in the charge of a bellboy in a red jacket and a pillbox hat. She hadn't seen the lobby of the hotel yet, since the cab brought her to a side entrance where her baggage could be put directly on an elevator. Refusing to let the bellboy take the leaden case, she followed him down the corridor and out into an immense hall four stories high and as broad as the Paris Opera. She stopped, stunned at the spectacle.

The marble hall was hung with crystal chandeliers, arranged symmetrically around a larger one hanging in the center. Everything was marble, onyx, and mahogany. A crowd was milling around on the floor of the lobby. Some of the men were in business suits, others in shirtsleeves, but almost all of them wore Stetson hats with the brims turned up on the sides. Their attention was fixed on something on a platform in the center of the lobby, and then she made out what it was. The platform was of polished mahogany with a heavy steel railing around it. On it was standing an immense black animal with a bulky chest and short curved horns. Its mass was formidable. It must have weighed tons. It came to the shoulder of the attendant who was standing beside it, holding the rope that led to the ring in its nose and stroking it now and then to calm it. Its broad black head was lowered, and as she watched a crystal rope of saliva dropped slowly from its muzzle and sank to the floor. She thought this was the strangest sight she had seen yet in this bizarre country: this black and obtuse, primordial animal enthroned in this palace of crystal and mahogany.

"But what is it?" she asked the bellboy.

"It's the National Stock Show, Ma'am. That bull is a prize Angus. Worth a quarter of a million."

She could hardly believe what he was saying. Mechanically she translated the dollars into francs; the bull was worth as much as a gram of glowstone, as much as seventy tons of Stockhausen ore. She and the others had labored for months, for years, to produce their tiny fragment of phosphorescent metal, and this animal had come into being without effort as they worked, made of grass and air, an immense stinking idol with beady eyes, a God of Meat. No wonder these men had set him up in this palace and worshiped him, standing about in their strange hieratic hats.

After she had refreshed herself and changed—which meant changing her underwear, since she put the black serge dress back on again—she locked the leaden case to the frame of the bed with a chain and padlock. Then she went down to dinner in the dining room, which was also large, with mahogany paneling and tables gleaming with white linen and crystal. She had refused a dinner invitation from the society women, explaining that she was tired from the journey. She ordered a little white meat of chicken with steamed vegetables. Offered wine, she asked for an herbal tea instead. The waiter brought her a pot of camomile, while the other diners craned their heads to see what this strange woman was doing. Americans, she began to see, took an immense interest in other people's affairs and didn't respect one's privacy at all. Finally came an apple, which she peeled in the way she had been taught by her mother, impaling it on a fork and then going round and round with the knife so that an even and unbroken spiral of skin was left on the plate.

All conversation stopped at several tables around while the diners watched this. Claire was aware of them but couldn't be bothered. She was sure of herself and confident in her own ways, and didn't intend to change her customs to suit those in a barbaric country where people ate potatoes with their skins on and gnawed corn from the cob. She cut the apple into six segments, chopped these neatly into morsels, and ate them with a knife and fork. Probably, she thought, they had expected her to seize it unskinned and bite into it like a barge boy.

When she finished dinner it was about nine o'clock. She was

still stiff from the train journey and she thought she might take a walk; the city had seemed safe enough from the glimpses she had had of it from the cab. When she went through the lobby she saw that the Angus bull was gone; there was only a placard advertising his qualities and a lingering stench of the barnyard. She went out into the dark city illuminated with gas lamps. The streets were as square as the farms on the prairie; they were all alike and intersected exactly at right angles. at this hour the shops were dark and gloomy. Perhaps this city, which she had never seen before, was the model of her Geographic Dream. There was a smell of something odd in the air, a scent of grass from the prairie, or possibly the smell of cattle greatly diluted; she had noticed that even unpleasant odors like musk became oddly savory when they were faint.

She went down a street some distance from the hotel, observing that she had strayed into a poorer part of town. In the light of the gas lamp there scratched along toward her a dog so thin that he was like a cage on four wooden pegs; he opened his mouth and grinned at her as she passed. There was mud on the sidewalk here, even though the rest of the city was clean. Passing under a gas lamp went two women with tight dresses and berouged faces. They had no coats but seemed no more conscious of the cold than the dog. As they passed she heard them laugh, a little tinkle that was swallowed up in the dark. A smell of whiskey came from an open doorway. From another doorway, no, it was an alley, a narrow passage between two buildings, emerged a man in a cheap cloth cap and a threadbare coat. He was bent forward in the middle like a semaphore and he had his hand extended toward her with the palm up. He shuffled toward her while her heart pounded.

"Sister, can you spare a dime?"

He watched her with his mournful eyes as she turned and fled back the way she had come. She had some difficulty finding her hotel again. The dark streets stretched away endlessly, they were all alike, and she was afraid to ask the men standing in front of buildings for directions. For an hour or more she wandered up one block and down the other, catching sight of a familiar storefront or advertising sign but unable to remember where it was in relation to the hotel. Perhaps she could dream her way back to the Brown Palace. Finally she saw it ahead of her, standing like a ship with its prow cleaving the darkness.

Her lecture the next afternoon was a considerable success. The people who filled the ballroom of the Brown Palace were mainly laymen; there was no university in Denver and only a few scientists had come from the state university in Boulder City. When the room was darkened there was a respectful silence as she showed the phosphorescent tube, and the trick of the electroscope and the magic lantern produced a round of applause. After the lecture she chatted with her American sponsors, spoke briefly with the professors from Boulder, and showed her tube of glowstone to anyone who wanted to see it. Several children were allowed to hold it in their hands, laughing at the blue-green glow that curved around their fingers. The professors, like those in Philadelphia, stood off and looked dubious as the others handled the sample. With a stiff little smile Claire showed them the scars on her fingers. "You needn't be afraid of the risk, gentlemen. I've worked with such materials for years and it's only done this."

By the time everyone had dispersed it was five o'clock in the afternoon. Claire went up to her room, which was large and luxuriously appointed, in dark polished wood with brass fittings. She planned to bathe, go down to dinner, and then retire early; her train for New York left the next morning. She got down on her hands and knees and chained the leaden case to the bedframe with a large brass lock, the key to which she slipped into the pocket of her dress.

At the moment she stood up there was a knock on the door. "Who is it?"

"The bellboy, Ma'am."

"What do you want?" She was a little annoyed; she was tired and she was longing for her bath.

"There's a letter for you. From France."

She opened the door and took it from him, recognizing the beige envelope of the Institute. Her first thought was that something had gone wrong in the laboratory, that there had been some sort of an accident. She opened it and found it was from Lancelot. He filled three whole pages with his small precise hand, which resembled that of a dutiful schoolgirl who had recently been studying Greek. There was a hieratic cast to certain of the letters, peculiar to Lancelot, that made it difficult to read. Frowning, she sat down and puzzled it out.

Well, it was nothing much. He wrote to say there was no news. Turning the envelope over and examining the postmark, she saw it had been written just a day or two after his return to Paris. It had caught up with her because of the three days she had spent in Princeton and Philadelphia. "Dearest Claire, my beloved colleague . . ." On and on. He reported that he had brought Hermine safely back to Paris and delivered her to the apartment, leaving her in the capable charge of the concièrge Mme Lacrosse. "On the voyage from London to Paris, which is certainly not without its perils for an innocent young girl, I saw to her safety and decorum with diligence." So he expressed himself. All this hardly needed saying. It was to be expected. If he had *not* seen to her safety and decorum, if he had attempted to violate her in the train, then that would have been news. She sighed and went on.

The second page was devoted to details of the work of the Institute, mainly a review of things that Claire already knew, since Lancelot had been back in the laboratory only for a day or two when he wrote the letter. These interested her, though, and she frowned, making notes on the edge of the paper with a pencil.

When she turned to the last page the style of the letter changed abruptly. It became personal and adulatory, swelling with its own dignity and with the respect he professed for Claire and her lifetime of work in the Institute. He confessed the pride he felt in having been allowed to work at her side, and his sense of privilege in the fact that he had, at least in some respects, been admitted to the duties and responsibilities of her late lamented husband.

"As you know I have never married. My whole life in recent

years has been devoted to my work in the Institute. A man wishes to leave behind him some offspring to perpetuate his name in posterity; it is a deep instinct and a universal one. That satisfaction is denied me. But I have a child, and it is one I share with you and our colleagues in the Institute; it is that glowing element which we have given together to the world, and which is destined to go forth over the earth to offer its" (or "his"; the pronoun was the same in French) "boon to all mankind. It is in this that I take my pride, and it is in this that the deepest impulses of my being find their final expression and fulfillment."

She smiled, finding that he had gone a little too far in his obstetrical metaphor, but her eyes were moist and she dabbed at them with her handkerchief. He was a fool, but such a loyal and devoted one; he had been Paul's friend and closest associate, and he was fond of her too and she of him. She put away her handkerchief, mocking herself at her own tears. Sitting down at the walnut writing desk, she took hotel stationery, pen, and ink from the drawer. As she wrote she found herself, through emotion of some kind of contagion, falling into his own style.

> My dear Lancelot. Words cannot tell how your letter moved and consoled me. Solitary as I am, totally alone in the vast spaces of this foreign continent, it brought a tear to my eye to read your expression of devotion to me and to what we both hold dear. And now, the child we have made together I bear with me here in America, in this distant land. How many hours have we isolated ourselves from the world, in the privacy of our companionship, to produce at last this precious consummation! The day will come when mankind recognizes this precious boon, the promise of salvation for the sufferings and ignorance of man. With total affection, from a far land, I am, dear Lancelot, your devoted friend Claire.

She sealed the envelope, addressed it, and looked around the room for a stamp. Never mind, the bellboy would have one. She was so tired that she hardly remembered what she had written.

GLOWSTONE

* * *

She was in the act of undressing for her bath when there was a knock on the door, then in the next instant the door opened and a figure in white slipped into the room. She thought at first it was someone from the hotel staff, another example of American casualness. She was indignant; she hastily rebuttoned the collar of the black dress.

Instead it was a tall man in a white linen suit and a black string tie, holding in his hands a hat with a broad brim. She faced him stiffly, her fingers still at the throat of her dress.

He seemed about to withdraw, then changed his mind, came in, and closed the door behind him. "How do you do, Mrs. Savarin-Decker. I'm Blanco White. It's really an honor to make your acquaintance. I must say, I had heard of you in advance, but when I saw you give your lecture in the ballroom this afternoon it was a revelation. From where I was sitting in the rear of the room I couldn't see you very well. But I don't know whether you've noticed that when you do that demonstration with the magic lantern your own profile is projected on the screen about ten feet high. When I saw that outline something in me was profoundly stirred. I knew that something important had happened to me and that my life would be different from now on."

She stared at him and he smiled apologetically. "Stendhal," he went on, "speaks of this process in his treatise on Love; he calls it crystallization."

"Stendhal?"

"He means that each of us carries in himself—he was speaking chiefly of men, he was a terrible egotist, I'm afraid—a kind of network of capabilities for love, unformed and tentative, and that sometimes if you're lucky, you encounter another person, perhaps in some accidental way, and all these capabilities suddenly solidify into a pattern of attraction so powerful that it seems almost a blow of fate, something super, natural; and that is what we mean by falling in love."

She wondered if she could get around him to the button of the electric bell to summon someone from the hotel, but it was on the opposite side of the room. "Mr.—I didn't catch your name."

"The profile I saw on the screen was that of a young girl—I know you're not a young girl, but I'm telling you what I saw—a young girl of classical beauty who combined in some subtle way the spirit of America with that of Europe. If I'm not mistaken, you're partly of European parentage and partly of American."

"You read that in the program for the lecture."

He grinned. "Well, I may have. But I think I might have guessed it even without the program. The outline that I saw on the screen was as subtle and perfect as that of a Grecian urn. Certain works of art have the power to affect us in that way, stirring something powerful and inchoate in us without our being quite able to say how it's done—a line of a Japanese drawing, a cornice of the Parthenon. That was the impression the profile had on me. Meanwhile," he went on, "as I was staring at the shadow on the screen, you were explaining, in your voice with its delightful trace of some European accent or other, these extremely complex matters of the discovery of glowstone, so that at the same time I was impressed with your scientific knowledge and your mastery of a very difficult subject. Under the influence of these two powerful impressions, the visual and the intellectual, Stendhal's crystallization took place in me in a single instant. It was a coup de foudre. You'll have to excuse my French; I speak it well enough but my accent is poor."

He was evidently some kind of eloquent madman. She glanced again at the bell button on the wall, but he was standing directly in front of it, blocking her way. "You say you gathered all this from seeing my shadow in the magic lantern?"

"That's right. You may think it's odd that so important a thing could happen through the influence of what was only a shadow. But all we're ever allowed to see of the world is its shadow, images on the retina of the eye. We're Plato's captives in the cave, condemned to tell what we can about the world from the flickering lights on the wall in front of us. We can never turn around and see what's really causing the flickers.

If we did, perhaps it would be too much for us; we couldn't bear it."

She drew away from him a little, and unconsciously her hands went again to the collar of her dress.

"That's the same dress you wore at the lecture, isn't it? And I saw you wearing it in the dining room last night."

This reminded her to be angry again. "What right have you to make remarks on my costume? And why have you come bursting in on me like this?"

"Why, I knocked and nobody answered, so I thought I'd see for myself if you were in. I tried to induce the hotel manager to introduce us, but he's a man of limited imagination, I'm afraid. May I sit down? I'll only stay a minute. I do have something to tell you, though." He took one of the cretonne-covered armchairs and set his hat on the other.

Since there was no other place to sit, Claire sat down on the bed and examined him more carefully. He was tall like so many men in the American West, with broad shoulders and large hands and feet. His features were even and he had iron-blue eyes. The lower part of his face was chapped from the wind and sun. Farther up, where his hat usually covered it, his forehead was pale as alabaster. His hair was luxuriant and molded as if it were sculpted in some solid substance; it was silver in color but this didn't seem to indicate age. He didn't give the impression of a young man or an old man, simply a man. The fact that his hair was silver was of no significance in determining his age, any more than the fact that Apollo has hair which is marble or bronze is of any use in establishing his age. It simply establishes that he is Apollo. He sat in the armchair with his hands on his knees, politely watching her while she collected her wits to decide what to say to him.

"What is it you want of me?"

"Why, I merely want the favor of your acquaintance, Mrs. Savarin-Decker. I don't ask anything of you at all. Perhaps you'll allow me to make you a little gift I have in mind. That's what I've come to talk to you about. But if you say the word I'll get up this minute and go away." He hesitated for a fraction of a second, but she said nothing and he went on. "You see, I'm a great admirer of the fair sex in general. I have been all my life. I enjoy all the fine things the world has to offer—art, music, good food, conversation—and among these the pleasure of female company is surely one of the finest and most uplifting. I've known a great many women, I'll confess to you quite frankly, but I must say I admire you more than any woman I've ever seen. When I caught sight of that shadow in the light of the magic lantern, Mrs. Savarin-Decker, I fell head over heels in love with you, and I expect to remain the same for the rest of my life."

"Oh, stop calling me Mrs. Savarin-Decker."

"All right. What do you want me to call you?"

"Most people who are not close friends address me as Madame."

He made his grin again. "I couldn't call you that. That means something else in Colorado. Suppose I call you Claire."

She was startled. "How did you know that was my name?"

"Why, it's printed right on the program. Everybody knows it's your name."

"That doesn't make it any better. You still oughtn't to call me that. So soon." And then she was angry with herself for having inadvertently added these last two words. They were both silent for a moment. He was still sitting in the armchair with a hand on each knee, gazing at her with a glance that, she was sure, was fixed on the buttons of her dress. She found herself in a state of curious ambivalence. Her indignation at this callous invasion of her privacy was as strong as ever, yet something prevented her from pressing the button of the electric bell or ordering him summarily from her presence. It was partly a curiosity about what he had to say, but it was also a more complicated fascination with his white-clad person, his lanky casualness, his Western twang in which he nevertheless referred to Plato and to French authors she had never heard of. It was with a sense of deep guilt that she allowed him to stay—but only for a few moments, she told herself. He seemed at least to be a gentleman—of the sort they had in the American West—and he would surely leave if she told him flatly to go. If not, there was always the electric bell. It never occurred to her to fear for her chastity, even though on another level she had the distinct sense that it was precisely her femininity that she and he were discussing, along with her intellectual attainments; but these too, he seemed to imply, were admirable precisely because they were the attainments of a woman with a classical profile. No one had ever spoken to her in this manner in her life.

Finding herself lost in these thoughts, she was exasperated with herself. "You said you had something to tell me. Why don't you say what it is and then you can go."

"Just as you like. You see, I have a good many interests here in Colorado. I was born here and I've spent most of my life in the state, although sometimes I go out to stay at the Del Coronado in California, and I often go to Europe in the season. I've never married; I never found the right woman. I have a ranch in the southern part of the state near Alamosa. I inherited the ranch from my family. It's a cattle ranch, as a matter of fact. It's not a business to interest a learned woman like you. I also have other interests, including some silver mines in the mountains up by Telluride. They tell me the tailings give off steam or something, or that you can see them in the dark. I don't understand it myself. I thought they might be useful to you. They're certainly no use to me. They're what you throw away after you've refined the silver out of the ore."

"The Telluride ores!"

"Yes, that's the little gift I had in mind."

"Then you're Mr. White!"

"I told you my name. I wrote you a letter to your Paris address, but perhaps it's slipped your mind. You don't have to buy the ore from those bandits in Transylvania. I'll give it to you free, and I'll even pay for shipping it to Paris. Money's no object; I don't know what to do with mine half the time. I'd be happy to donate the whole pile of dirt to you in the cause of science. Anyhow, I'm so struck with you that I'd give you the whole world and the shirt off my back if you asked me. I'll tell you what. Here's my proposal, which you've been waiting for with such curiosity. Why don't I leave you for an hour while you change into your evening dress, and then we'll go out to dinner and settle this business of the Telluride ores. You don't have to dine here in your hotel. We can go to Maxim's. It's not Maxim's in Paris, but it's the best restaurant in Denver."

"I don't have an evening dress. This is the only dress I have. I don't care to go out to dinner. The food in the hotel is quite adequate. I'm not very interested in food anyhow. As far as I can see, it's just a fuel that you take in from time to time so that you can go on working. It's not considered proper, in the circles I move in, for a widow to dine with an unmarried gentleman, and it's also not proper for a lady to entertain a gentleman in her room in a hotel with no one else present. I'm grateful for your interest, even for your—admiration," she said lamely, her cheeks warming, "but these are not the circumstances in which to talk about mine tailings and ores. Simply write me a letter in Paris explaining your proposal, and I'll take it up with my associates."

But even as she said this, she found herself coveting this new and unknown American earth with its strange name, and she also had mixed feelings about this white-clad giant who burst into her room without being invited and yet treated her with the courtesy of a natural nobleman, even though with the lanky casualness that seemed to afflict all Americans. She was a little sorry now that she had declined his invitation so abruptly. Perhaps someone could be found to go along as chaperon; but who, in this city in which she knew no one but him?

"I'm grateful," she told him a little stiffly, "for the offer to donate the Telluride ores without cost."

"And I'm grateful to you, Mrs. Savarin-Decker, for the pleasure of your acquaintance. Perhaps sometime later you'll allow me to call you Claire."

She went down to dinner a little after eight and found the dining room almost empty; Americans dined earlier than Europeans and most of the guests had finished their meal and left. She sat down and began studying the menu, and then noticed something moving at the edge of her vision. She looked up and found a trio of waiters making their way toward her across the room.

Without explaining themselves they set their burdens down. First came a gigantic basket of roses, so large that it covered the table and made it difficult to see around it, and then a bottle of champagne in a silver bucket on a stand. The third waiter carried a Pomeranian puppy, with as much dignity as he could muster under the circumstances. He set this on the chair next to her at the table: a small spot of fluff with two black eyes and a button nose at one end. Under the puppy he put the napkin in which he had carried it. The creature blinked at her out of its small glistening eyes and made no effort to get down off the chair.

Looking around the room, she found Blanco White seated at a table across the room facing in her direction. She felt an annoyance that quickly grew to a hot resentment, mainly because she didn't know how to behave before the waiters in these circumstances. Mechanically, scarcely realizing what she was doing, she broke off a rosebud and pinned it to the bodice of her dress.

He took this as a sign and got up and came to her table. He carried his cream-colored hat in his hand; he seemed as unable to separate himself from it as a mother is from a baby. "Good evening, Mrs. Savarin-Decker. It's a shame that a wonderful woman like you should have to dine alone. This champagne is from France so it should make you feel at home." He said nothing about the roses. He just smiled on them, as if his trick of producing roses from the prairie in November was nothing special, just something an ordinary magician would do in the course of a day's work. He pulled out a chair, turned it around, and sat down with his legs straddling it. In this way he was present at the table but only as a spectator, so to speak, a patron; he had not yet joined it as a guest. His hat he set on the fourth chair; the other three were occupied by Claire, the Pomeranian, and himself. Finding that she was hidden from his view by the roses, he made a sign to the waiter. The fellow understood immediately what he wanted, and hurried up with a wicker flower stand on which he arranged the roses at the other side of the table. Another waiter was already uncorking the champagne, and a third brought a small platter of caviar with tiny squares of bread.

"I don't eat very much. All this is unnecessary."

"Of course it is. It's the unnecessary things in the world that make life worth living. As Voltaire puts it, 'Le superflu, chose si nécessaire.' They knew how to live in the eighteenth century. That was the best time to be alive, I think. Of course, after them came the Revolution, but Voltaire was dead by that time. I've taken the liberty," he said, "of ordering dinner for you. The food in the Brown Palace is all right but it's nothing to write home about. I've had Alphonse, the chef from Maxim's Restaurant, come over to supervise your dinner. We can't offer you what you have in Paris but Alphonse is not so bad. He's not a real Frenchman; he's from New Orleans. I hope you won't mind if I join you."

Without waiting for an answer he turned the chair around, sat down in it, and pulled it up to the table. "Here, have a little caviar. It's the best Beluga."

He took one of the postage-stamp-sized pieces of bread, buttered it, piled a cone of caviar on it, and passed it to her on a plate. His hands were the same deep tan as his cheeks, and his wrists where they protruded from his sleeves were thick and pale, with tiny hairs that seemed blue. She took the plate and instead of setting it down nibbled cautiously at the edges of the square of bread. She had never tasted caviar. It had three qualities. It tasted fishy, it was far too salty, and it was delicious. Without realizing what she was doing she took a sip of champagne from her goblet, which had been filled by the waiter. She had never had champagne before either. As the sparkling little stars spread under her tongue and sank down into her chest she realized there was an insidious trap here, one that had very likely been planned by Blanco White. Caviar was so salty that it made you want to drink something afterward, and the characteristic of champagne was such that it made her immediately want to eat caviar. She pushed the goblet away, and the next time he offered her the caviar she left it untouched on the plate.

If he noticed this he paid no attention. "You haven't said whether you'll allow me to join you for dinner, so I take it I have your permission. If you say so I'll go away and you can enjoy the dinner by yourself. I certainly don't intend to make a nuisance of myself. I respect you too much for that. I'll be content," he said perfectly cheerfully, "if I'm just allowed to look at you with my lovesick eyes, and if possible to tag along behind you a little bit. Like your pet dog, you might say. This animal," he said, taking up the Pomeranian gently in his tanned hands, "is named Boris. He has his name engraved on this silver plate on his collar, and your name too. I expect he'll be grateful if you take him back to Paris with you. Most dogs that he could associate with around here are a good deal larger and more ferocious than Boris. He's six months old and he belonged to a friend of mine. I thought of him as soon as I laid eyes on your face."

"I couldn't possibly be bothered with a dog."

"It's a very small one. If he's left here in Denver I expect the other dogs will rend him limb from limb." He put Boris back on the chair where he resumed his blinking. A pink tongue appeared, and he looked from one to the other as the conversation went on. Claire found herself staring at the hat on the fourth chair. It was the color of vanilla ice-cream, it was spotless, and it had a black ribbon around it as fine as one on a lady's dress. The curve of the brim was extraordinarily subtle. It dipped down in front and back, and on the sides it rose up in an arc of mathematical precision. She tried to remember what such a shape was called. It was an anticlastic curve, she thought, a form of hyperbola, but three-dimensional and perhaps not finite.

"Is your name really Blanco White?"

"Well, you know," he said with his easy grin, "nothing really has a name. We call things what they seem to us. I call myself what I seem to me, and so my name is Blanco."

"And you always wear white clothing," she murmured. "It must get soiled so quickly."

"Everybody else's clothes get dirty too, but they don't notice it because they're dark. As soon as I see a smudge on my suit

I get it cleaned. I've got four of them, exactly alike. How does it happen that you're named Claire?"

"Why, I don't know. It's just my name."

"It means light in French, of course. A ray of light. It's just the right name for you. Claire de lune. Do you know Debussy's little nocturne?" He tucked a portion of caviar into his mouth, evidently with relish, and washed it down with a sip of champagne.

"I didn't choose my name. It's just one my parents gave me," she told him a little distantly. "I don't think they had anything in particular in mind."

He only smiled at this. The champagne and caviar were taken away and the dinner ordered by Blanco proceeded, served by the trio of efficient waiters. First came brook trout lightly sautéed in butter with watercress, and then sweetbreads in a thin mauve-colored sauce with capers and dill. There was a white Moselle with the trout and a rosé with the sweetbreads. These wines too Claire only touched to her lips and then pushed the glasses away.

"Alphonse is a reasonably good cook," Blanco was saying. "He and I went on a fishing trip together last spring, at Grand Lake in the Rockies. It's beautiful country up there. I wish you could see it. I showed him how to cook trout. We carried along a little butter with us and the cress you get right from the creek. Never roll it in cornmeal, I told him. That's the way they do it in New Orleans where he comes from. Trout has a delicate flavor and you mustn't overpower it. Then we went down to the ranch at Alamosa and he showed me how to cook sweetbreads. The secret of it is that the sauce is made from black beans, cooked until they're soft and then puréed. You wouldn't think that black beans would make a sauce violet-colored, but they do. We had to slaughter twelve calves to get the sweetbreads, but it was worth it. The rest of the meat went to the hands."

She had to smile at this. She began to see that what might be taken in another person, a European, for boasting—that he had so much money that he didn't know how to spend it, that he slaughtered twelve calves for a dish of sweetbreads—was merely a naive stating of the facts. He declared himself with absolute candor on everything, including his alleged infatuation with Claire herself, and yet she had the impression that she still knew nothing whatsoever about him. He was like a little boy telling you that he had a red wagon or that he very much wanted an ice-cream. Were all Americans like that, she wondered? If they were, perhaps this was the very simple answer to what seemed to them, to Europeans, a complicated question, how they could be as simple and guileless as children and yet go about the world doing exactly as they pleased, exterminating the Indians with stops for prayers, seizing Panama from the Colombians and building the Canal, claiming to have invented the aeroplane when it was really invented by Blériot. Blanco was as incapable of boasting as a three-year-old child. She tried to remember whether her own father was like this. She thought not.

The sweetbreads and rosé were taken away—Claire had eaten almost nothing—and were followed by fruit, cheese, and pastries. She would never have imagined that such a complicated menu was possible in Denver, but then Alphonse was from New Orleans.

Blanco fed a piece of cheese to Boris, whose mouth was so tiny that one's little finger would hardly fit into it. "Would you care for a cup of coffee? Alphonse makes it in the New Orleans way, roasted with chicory and black as sin. I've tried to show the boys down at the ranch how to make it, but they won't touch the stuff. Cowboys are particular about coffee. They won't drink it unless it's made in an old tin can."

"Are you going back to your ranch soon?"

"Oh, I've made up my mind to follow you back to Paris. If it's not an impertinence. What time does your train leave tomorrow? I often go to Europe in November anyhow, and this way I can escort you across the country at the same time. You know, this is the West after all. A woman shouldn't travel around in it by herself. I'd be happy to go along and protect you from the attentions of anybody you didn't want to meet."

And who is going to protect me from you, she thought. "I have no intention of telling you what time my train leaves. It's a completely impossible idea for you to follow me back to France. I forbid it categorically. I can't hear of it." She was in a mild panic now, thinking of Hermine, Lancelot, and the others in the laboratory, and of the prurient and probing French journalists. "You don't seem to realize that I'm a woman of a certain age and a widow; I have a daughter who's almost grown. I'm a scientist and my whole life is in my laboratory; I don't have time for dallying around. Perhaps you do. You don't seem to have much else to do but wear white suits and prowl around in hotels after women you haven't been introduced to. The whole thing is preposterous. I can't be responsible for your ridiculous infatuations. You yourself said that you fell in love with a shadow from the magic lantern."

"Oh, I admit that I'm a queer specimen. It's very likely that I'm crazy; the poets themselves say that love is a form of madness. You'll just have to take me as I am. I don't demand anything of you at all. As a matter of fact there's only one train leaving for New York tomorrow. If you don't mind, I'll just tag along behind you, like Boris. If anyone tries to be rude to you I'll fix his wagon quickly enough. We're not responsible for our nature, and that's just the way I'm made. A knight in armor, you might say. Or one of those medieval poets who sang under ladies' windows. I'm a romantic."

In the ornate iron cage of the elevator—a queer word to use instead of the English lift, it suggested something elevating or elevated, almost a religious idea, and this seemed to her typically American—Claire had to admit quite privately to herself that it was pleasant to dine with someone else, even though she was still a little uneasy about the dubious circumstances of their encounter. No one in France must know of this, she told herself. He can send his ores if he wishes and I'll thank him politely by letter. If he attempts to follow me onto the train I'll have him put off by the porters. I am not the kind of woman who—who what? She didn't finish the thought. She wasn't quite sure what dubious consequences might result from her *not* rejecting Blanco's elaborate and naive curlicues of admiration. He himself said that he expected nothing from her. Why should she be afraid of giving him nothing? Then something clutched at her heart like a quick hand of ice, like a dark shadow rearing up at her suddenly on a deserted street, and she gasped out loud, "Paul!"

She had a private compartment on the train, a small room paneled in hardwood with gilded decorations, identical to the one that had carried her from Philadelphia to Denver. It contained an armchair, a divan, a writing desk, a bed that came down from overhead, and a washbasin that folded up and disposed of its contents into a reservoir somewhere underneath the train. One window looked out into the passing landscape, the other onto the corridor of the Pullman car. There were lace curtains with tassels on the windows and a small glass bud vase on the wall. Into this she put the rose she had fastened to her dress the night before, even though it was a little wilted. On the floor at her feet was the leaden case, and on the divan beside her was Boris, who looked around at everything brightly but calmly as though he was quite accustomed to trains. She too felt at home in the compartment with its elegant but efficient furnishings, although she didn't look forward to the eighteen hours of crawling over the interminable prairies to Chicago.

Boris had perfect manners, except that he burst out into his yippy bark when anyone entered the compartment. But he didn't bark at Blanco. Blanco (as she called him in her mind now, although she didn't yet say it out loud) had managed to get a compartment in the same car as hers, although at the other end. It was piled almost full with his white leather luggage, and in it he sat on the divan with his feet on the suitcases, smoking a cheroot as long and thin as a lead pencil and watching the landscape go by. He wouldn't have dreamed of smoking in the presence of a lady. Like Boris he had perfect manners. He allowed at least an hour to go by after the train left Denver, until it was out in the wheat fields of eastern Colorado, before he came down the car to Claire's compartment.

Up to this moment she hadn't known he was on the train. He lifted his hat and opened the door a crack. "Excuse me, I don't want to intrude, but if you'd care for a little chat I'd be glad to accommodate you. This is pretty boring country. Once you've seen one wheat field you've seen them all. I can't think what you do in here all by yourself. Of course you have Boris. But one is grateful for a little human company once in a while too. However, it's entirely up to you."

As a matter of fact she had been making notes for her article on the loss of weight in glowstone. She sighed and closed her eyes. He took this as a sign of permission, slipped in through the door, set his hat on the floor, and sat down in the armchair. The compartment seemed much smaller with his long lanky form in it. Even though his chair was against the opposite wall his outstretched ankles almost touched her feet.

In silence they watched the featureless prairie unroll past the window. There was a line of telegraph poles along the track, and Claire's eye was caught by the wires that staggered down as they left each pole and then swooped up again, like a flock of terrified birds, to rush through the next pole on the line. This induced vertigo. She turned from the window and found herself staring at Blanco's tanned cheeks, his alabaster brow, and his blue eyes which had crow's-feet at the sides as deep as though cut with a knife.

When their glances met she looked away in confusion and laid her hand absentmindedly on Boris. It was the first time she had touched him. Up to this point he had been handled entirely by waiters and Pullman porters. She was irrationally surpised to find the small body warm; she had thought of it as something like a toy for children. Boris produced his small pink tongue and panted, and Blanco smiled.

"You're going home. And Boris is going to Europe for the first time. What a fortunate dog." He reached out and touched his head, and Boris glanced at his mistress as if to point out the significance of this ritual. A small dog is an ambassador, she thought. I pet it, he pets it, and there's a link between us, even though we two haven't touched at all. How was it, she asked herself, that he had persuaded her to accept this animal?

"And I feel fortunate too," he rattled on, "in being allowed to trail along after you, carrying your grip and fending off unwanted attention from mashers and other unprincipled people. This is the Wild West, Claire. It's no place for a woman traveling alone."

"I didn't give you permission to trail along after me. And I don't believe the West is as wild as that. It looks like perfectly ordinary farm country."

"I wonder if you've noticed that there are some very dubious characters on this train. One of them I'm practically sure is a well-known train robber. However, if anything out of the way happens you can count on me to see to your interests."

"Oh, nonsense." She had to laugh.

He smiled too, and examined her face with a kind of curiosity. Then he dropped his facetious manner and became more serious. "Look at this country, Claire." A cluster of silos went by, then a farmhouse with a rusty iron roof. A boy with a red chapped face, carrying his lunch in a tin workman's pail, stared at the train as it passed. "Compare this with the view from a train window in Europe, say on the journey between Le Havre and Paris. A countryside that looks like a park, well-kept farms, villages, church steeples, châteaux, rivers and canals with barges on them. Color, life. An old civilization with a history, a past."

She listened with a trace of her smile still on her lips, surprised at this new vein of seriousness in him. He paused and went on.

"I'm a thoroughgoing American. I don't think anybody is more American than I am. But this is a raw new country, Claire." His eyes were fixed on the prairie going by and not on her. "Big and gawky and so clumsy that it falls all over itself when it tries to walk. America is that boy we saw just now out of the train window, a kid in homespun clothes just come to town who doesn't know how to kiss a lady's hand. We need Europe to give us polish. We're all just misplaced Europeans here in America whether we know it or not. All our culture comes from across the Atlantic, everything that makes life more pleasurable than it is for a savage—art, music, literature, history, law. Architecture—the bank in every American town is an imitation Greek temple. We may believe that America is the best country in the world, but when we get rich we build ourselves mansions that look like English country houses."

"Your universities look like gothic castles," she said, remembering the hall where she had lectured at the University of Pennsylvania. She had an impulse to tell him about the young physicist who rode a bicycle, but she wasn't quite sure what the point of it was, except that the physicist had found an efficient way of getting to work using the power of his own body. "Americans are a practical people. This is an excellent train. They're very good with all kinds of gadgets and inventions."

"Yes. A practical people." He turned away from the window, but instead of looking at her he looked at Boris. "When I'm in Colorado I'm like the rest of them; I look after my cows and my mines. But every so often I get weary of the mud, the endless distances with the air so clear you can see things a hundred miles away, the tobacco-spitting, the shabby clothes, the tin storefronts, the blizzards that come down from Canada, these wheat fields that stretch on far too long. When I feel that way I do what a lot of other Americans do; I go to Europe to recover my past. I go to galleries and study the paintings of the great masters, I visit cathedrals and castles, I go to concerts to hear Mozart and Wagner—you can hardly hear Wagner in America unless you go to New York or Chicago."

"There are phonographs now."

"That's it exactly. Europe is a performance of *Die Götterdämmerung* in Bayreuth, and America is a phonograph. A lame squeaky imitation of the real thing."

"I think you're too hard on your country. There are many fine people in it and the mountains are magnificent. You called me Claire several times, by the way. I didn't give you permission for that either."

"Claire, I've got to tell you something about myself. I wouldn't bother you with it except that it will explain to you why it is I'm on this train on my way to Paris instead of at my ranch at Alamosa tending to my business." When she said nothing and waited expectantly he went on. "When I was a small boy I used to have a reverie about a beautiful woman clad in black who would come into my room and stand by my bed. Her face was pale and silvery and she had beautiful dark eyes. In my thoughts I called her the Silver Lady. She was like a goddess or a princess, and after a while she would smile and beckon me to follow her across the sea to the palace where she lived. Do you know who that woman was, Claire?"

She gazed back at him fixedly.

"She was Europe, Claire. I don't know how I knew about Europe at that age. Probably I had seen pictures in a book or people had described it to me. But the Silver Lady was calling me to come and visit her in her palace. When I grew up and made a lot of money—a good deal of it in silver mines, by the way—I did go and visit her, and I've done it every year since. Now I'm going back to visit her in her palace again."

In spite of herself, Claire found herself annoyed that the Silver Lady was only a personification of Europe and not any specific person. The thought was unworthy of her and she reproached herself for allowing herself to get into a state of mind where such resentments were possible. It was a mistake to allow Blanco to speak to her of his absurd infatuations at all, she now saw. It was because she was alone, far from home in a foreign country, and he was at least someone to talk to. She would have done better to bring Lancelot and Hermine with her, or even Fabre, who could have worked the magic lantern for her and seen to her baggage. As she evoked these names everything in Paris came back to her in a flood, and she felt a panic at the predicament she had allowed herself to get into. She had promised herself that if he followed her onto the train she would have him put off by the porters; she hadn't done this, and instead she had allowed him to come into her compartment, a room where there was after all a bed, even though it was now folded up into the wall over her head.

The porter, a cheerful black man with a pink mouth, came down the corridor striking a set of chimes with a hammer. He opened the door of the compartment. "First call for lunch," he said. The door shut and he went off. The sound of the chimes receded.

"Blanco," she said firmly, "I wish to take my meal in the dining car alone."

Respectfully he unwound his long legs and got up. "It's been

very agreeable talking to you. I hope you found it the same."
He left with a bow, putting on his hat in the corridor.

During the rest of the trip to Chicago and on to New York
he came several times to sit with her for a chat. Sometimes she
leaned back on the divan and closed her eyes while he talked,
at other times she sat with her chin on her hand looking out
the window. It was difficult to get rid of him entirely, and
there was no point in doing so, since no one in Paris would
ever know about it. It was part of her experience in America,
she told herself. Once back in Paris she would take advice from
Lancelot on how to get rid of her awkward and ludicrous admirer, without telling him everything of course.

As the train left Colorado and passed on into Nebraska he
told her about his boyhood, about the excitement of coming
in from the country to be a student at the University of Colorado, about his year at Oxford where he read Greats but didn't
take his degree; he gave up his studies because his father died
and he had to come home to take care of the ranch. He told
her about his adventures hunting and fishing in the mountains with the boys from the ranch, and about his annual visits
to Europe; he was perfectly familiar with London, Paris, Rome,
and Vienna and sometimes made a pilgrimage to the Bayreuth Festival in the summer in addition to his winter trip. His
white linen suits were made in Chicago, and his hat came from
Dallas. He had a pocket watch in white gold with the inscrip-
tion "München" inside it when he opened the lid; he showed
it to her with a considerable satisfaction. She had to smile at
this. It's a nice red wagon, Blanco, she told him in her thoughts,
but you can't have an ice-cream. Sometimes after he had ram-
bled on for an hour or longer she would say, "I'm tired now,
Blanco, leave me," and he would. When this happened he went
back to his own compartment to smoke a cheroot and read for
a while. A little later she would see him pacing restlessly up
and down the corridor, looking into her compartment each
time he passed. If she turned her head away coldly he resumed his pacing; if she returned his glance he would open
the door and come in.

GLOWSTONE

Her rose was faded now and she threw it away. In a town called North Platte, Nebraska, a cluster of dreary unpainted houses on the prairie, Blanco got out to take Boris to answer a call of nature, as he called it, and came back with a meager cluster of marigolds tied with an orange string. He had wheedled them from the stationmaster's wife, who had them in a pot in her window. "I'm afraid that's all they have in this place," he said. He watched with the happiness of a little boy while she put them in the bud vase in the compartment.

IV

From Victoria station, Hermine and Lancelot were to travel
to Dover to take the Channel steamer to Calais, and from there
continue their way by another train to Paris. This three-step
journey, beginning at eleven in the morning at Victoria, would
bring them to the Gare du Nord at a little after nine in the
evening.

Lancelot was an old friend of the family and Hermine was
on familiar if somewhat distant terms with him. Even though
she had known him since she was a child, she still called him
Professor Lancelot and he called her Mademoiselle. He was a
loyal friend of her mother and had been particularly devoted
in his support at the time of the death of her father and the
troubled days that followed, a time that Hermine remembered
vividly even though with a certain haziness. Without the help
of Professor Lancelot, everyone said, Claire might well have
been unable to carry on with her work at the Institute under
the weight of the grief that oppressed her. Hermine imagined
that he was now a man of about forty; she was vague about

the ages of people in other generations. She had never before been alone with him for more than a few moments.

The carriage of the train was one of those with no corridor; the compartment, which seated eight, had a door at either end opening directly onto the platform when the train was stopped. It was empty now except for Hermine and Lancelot. It was late October in England and winter was already announcing itself; the air was gray and chilly with a smell of coal smoke, and in the compartment the lights were on. The train rattled on rhythmically through the muddy fields and gray villages of Kent. It was cold in the compartment. Lancelot had provided a steamer robe which was large enough to cover both of them if they sat close enough together. He had arranged it over Hermine's knees and then put his arm around her; it was the only comfortable place for the arm, since their shoulders touched under the robe. If she tried to move away from him, the robe slipped off and she crept back under his arm again. He was really very kind, and had been as solicitous of her welfare on the journey as he always was with her mother. The visit to England had been tiring for both of them. Now, with his head fallen back onto the little white napkin provided and his mouth slightly open, he dozed. Perhaps he wasn't really asleep; his eyes were closed and he seemed sunk in the profoundest thought.

She examined him as well as she could from so close a range; his head was only a foot from hers. If you study any human being closely, she reflected, especially when he is asleep, he seems ridiculous. Professor Lancelot was a man of medium height, of Alpine type as befitting his Grenoble origins. The chin was not the most prominent part of his features; it tended to disappear under the fold of his lower lip. His brow was broad and serene, and he was bald, she noticed, in a peculiar pattern, with a peninsula of hair along the center of his head which he combed down to the sides as best he could. The hair on top of his head was fine and silky, and the part of it that he attempted to comb to the sides had come unstuck at one place. She resisted an impulse to press it back onto the skull with her fingers.

Even though most of his body was covered by the steamer robe, she remembered his clothing perfectly, since like her mother he always wore the same thing. All dressed in black, with his wrinkled coattails and his lugubrious mien, he looked like an umbrella that somebody had forgotten at a picnic. Yet he had certain pretensions to elegance. His necktie he held in place with a diamond stickpin; he wore a black bowler, black silk socks with clocks, and polished black shoes, so gleaming that as they protruded from the steamer robe they reflected the lights overhead on the roof of the compartment. Hermine remembered what the Sisters had told her at school, that you should never dance with a man wearing patent-leather shoes, because he might use them as a mirror to look up your skirt. Lancelot's hat rested on the seat by his side, with a dent in it that he had tried to press out with his fingers. An aroma of eau de cologne hung over Lancelot, a scent of starched linen, and something else, faintly musky like the odor of a tomcat at dawn.

A set of curious farm structures went by; they were like windmills without their fans, and they had what looked like spouts or spigots at their tops. On the trip a few days before from Dover to London someone had told her that they were called oasthouses and had something to do with the curing of hops. The jiggling and jolting of the train made the steamer robe gradually slip down their bodies toward the floor. From time to time Lancelot adjusted it. She left these details to him; it was as though they were in a carriage and he was driving it. He was driving in his sleep, or with his eyes closed, but this made no matter. Since the air in the compartment was cold, they both left their hands under the robe, hers folded in her lap and his stretched out on his legs. When the robe slipped, he scratched at it from underneath until he had seized a fold of it and then pulled it back into place.

But this time his hands didn't return to his trouser legs; one of them did, but the other one came to rest on her leg. It was no doubt a mistake—he *was* almost asleep—but she hoped it was one he would correct. Instead, under the guise of adjusting the robe again, the hand rose up and descended on both

the legs, forcing a little piece of her dress into the ravine between them.

She glanced at him. Because of his slumped position his head
was lower than hers; his pink lids were closed over his eyes,
the stickpin rose and fell steadily with his breathing. The hand,
writhing slowly like some sea creature in an aquarium, insin-
uated itself a little farther into the crevice between her legs.

She murmured his name in a low voice, almost hesitant to
awaken him. In reply the hand began to creep up the legs
toward her body. Feeling a little strange herself, Hermine totally lacked a vocabulary to grasp what was happening. The
Sisters had spoken only of "that part of you," even the progressive lycée had ignored the subject, and her mother had
never referred to it at all. Hermine had two important reve-
lations. The first was that Professor Lancelot, even though
asleep, dozing, meditating, or wool-gathering, was unquestion-
ably, in some part of his mind or will, aware and therefore
responsible for what he was doing, that is molesting an unmarried girl who had been confided to his charge by her
mother. The other was that a perfectly innocent person like
herself could take a strange, dark, unknown, mysterious, warm,
and nectareous pleasure in being touched by a man twice her
age with a bald head, who smelled of cologne and starched
linen, and for whom she felt, if anything, a physical repulsion
rather than an attraction.

"Professor Lancelot!"

He fumbled, retracted his hands to his own midriff, and sat
up with a start. The steamer robe slid off them and he re-
trieved it, this time folding it and setting it on the seat beside
them.

"Mademoiselle. I must have been dozing."

"You must have. I think we're almost to Dover."

He gazed out the window at the farmhouses drifting by in
the mist. "Dover, of course, is in the county of Kent. Those
curious structures are called—"

"I know, oasthouses."

"You've been to England before?"

"No, but someone told me about them on the trip the other way. I love to travel. When I'm older I'd like to travel everywhere, all over the world. Not by myself, of course, but . . ." By a half-conscious association she added, "You've never married, Professor Lancelot."

He seemed to understand her perfectly, perhaps through some subliminal memory of his recent doze. "No. I've never found the right person. I have a great admiration for the fair sex. But when one is a scientist, you know, Mademoiselle, there isn't much time for one's personal satisfactions. The only women I've had occasion to meet are you and your mother. And of course Mlle Maedl at the laboratory." They both agreed implicitly that she was out of the question. "And in Grenoble, when I was a student, life was very limited."

Finding his coat unbuttoned, he buttoned it, and also extended his feet to see if the polish on his shoes had been damaged by his nap. After the recent revelation of his inner nature—his somnambulistic conduct—she didn't know what to call it—she looked out of the corner of her eye in a new way at the parts of him revealed by the removal of the steamer robe. His body, like his head, had a peculiar shape. His shoulders were narrow and his center of gravity was fixed somewhere below his waist. He had a small neat abdomen, not at all conspicuous. The thinness of his shoulders, the gentle curve that followed down his body to the round fundament perched on the train seat, suggested some rare fruit. Bilingual Hermine reflected that pear is a funny word when you are speaking French, but not at all in English. Whereas banana is funny in English but not in French. "Vieille poire," she murmured experimentally, almost inaudibly, to herself. Had he heard? She suppressed a smile.

When he spoke too his voice had pear-shaped tones, a kind of dulcet lilt, quite different from her father's laconic murmur with many clearings of the throat, as she remembered it. "If I may say so without impropriety, the woman who has played the greatest part in my own life up to this point, and the woman I've most admired, has been Madame. I have an enormous respect for your mother." He lightly stressed the *e* on the front of the word, as though he were making a phonetic demonstration: "un respect *é*-norme." He went on, "While remaining on the one hand thoroughly womanly, she has devoted herself to science with an energy, a tenacity, a spiritual vocation if I may say so, that few men could match. I express myself badly; I should have said that *no* man can match her except her husband, your departed father." He sighed and meditated over his memory of Paul Savarin. "There are few days in my life when I don't think of him—of his devotion to his work, of his genius as a scientist, of the tragedy of his being taken from us before his years were ripe." She had never listened to him carefully before, and she began to see that when he adopted this oratorical mode (he had dropped his intimacy now and was addressing her as though she were a funeral, or a public meeting) he always expressed himself in triads, so that his thoughts fell neatly into three parts. "But your mother stepped courageously into his shoes, and the work goes on. In the days of her greatest suffering she never flagged in her devotion to the work of the Institute. If in the future our cities are lighted by glowstone, if disease and suffering are banished, if we arrive finally at an understanding of the mystery of matter," (another triad) "we will owe it to this one courageous woman who pressed forward in her task in spite of the load of grief that lay on her heart." He thought over this, as though awed for a moment by his own eloquence, and then repeated, "I have an e-normous respect for her." It struck her that this burst of rhetoric that had come out of him had been triggered, from all evidence, by the accidental mention of her mother when he was still in an amorous mood occasioned by the fumbling under the steamer robe.

"And do you have a respect for me also, Professor Lancelot?"

He looked at her in surprise. "Why of course, Mademoiselle. I don't quite take your meaning. I have the greatest respect for all the fair sex. And further," he proceeded, groping for his own thought, "you're the child of your mother, and your father, the two people in the world that I've respected the most. So how could I not have respect for you?"

"But for me personally."

He still didn't quite follow her. "That goes without saying, Mademoiselle. I have an e-normous respect for you, as I have for your mother."

In Dover, while they were waiting to board the Channel steamer, there was a buffet with small metal tables to sit at and wire cane-bottomed chairs. Installing her at a table, he brought her a bowl of soup, a bun, and a piece of Cheshire cheese, along with a sandwich for himself. He ate carefully, brushing off the crumbs that fell onto his vest. From time to time he consulted his watch at the end of the gold chain to be sure they weren't late for the steamer. "In Paris it wouldn't be proper for us to be seen dining together. Of course this isn't dining but lunching, and no one knows us in Dover. I respect you enormously, Mademoiselle, as I do your mother. If you would like to refresh yourself before boarding the steamer, there is a special waiting room for ladies just over there. The facilities on the steamer are somewhat more primitive." He waited until she had disappeared, then he betook himself to the equivalent place for his own sex.

In Paris Hermine moved back into the empty apartment in Rue François-Villon. It was the first time she had been left alone for more than a day or two. When her parents had gone on lecture tours in Germany or Belgium, she had been sent to stay with her father's married sister in Place des Victoires. Now she was eighteen and sole mistress of the apartment, which all at once seemed enormous. Although she wasn't much of a cook, she could boil an egg or fry a cutlet for herself. Everything was an adventure. She could even have a little wine with her dinner if she wanted and no one would know. She exulted in her newfound freedom.

Following her mother's arrangements, the concièrge below in her loge served as duenna, but a very tolerant one. Mme Lacrosse, with her cat, her white apron, and her gold tooth, was the model of all Parisian concièrges; she might have been copied from a satirical drawing of the species in a newspaper. She sat all day long in her loge with her cat in her lap and her cup of tisane, looking out skeptically at the world, and getting most of her information about it from the Petit Parisien and other tabloids. She was a famous cynic and had an unlimited belief in the frailty of material substance. If something broke, if a water pipe sprang a leak or the cat had worms, she would say, "Que voulez-vous, Mademoiselle? It's the way of all flesh." A broom stood against the wall by her side but she never used it, as far as Hermine could see, and she never had the slightest curiosity about what Hermine was doing in the apartment all alone. As a matter of fact Hermine was doing very little and quickly became bored.

The reason she had been left alone in the apartment instead of going to stay with her aunt was that she was a student at the Sorbonne now, and the apartment was not far from her classes in the Faculty of Sciences. This first year she had lectures in chemistry and physics, and also a smelly laboratory session in which students demonstrated that if you heated sulphur and iron filings in a test tube it turned to ferric sulphate, a fact she had already learned in the lycée, so this part of it was easy for her. The mathematics, which was necessary for her chemistry course, was a little more formidable. This made her sigh sometimes. She realized she would never be a scientist like her parents if it involved the mastery of logarithms and calculus. What would she be then? She had no idea. For the moment she was a student at the Sorbonne, which was a pleasant enough thing to be.

Coming home one afternoon about a week after her classes had started, she first dumped her satchel of books, papers, and notebooks onto the kitchen table and drank a glass of water from the tap. It had a coppery taste and was a very light brown in color, a tint so faint that you would hardly notice it, but her mother always steadfastly maintained on scientific grounds that it was perfectly harmless and that buying mineral water was a waste of money. Then she went into the WC. This was a long narrow room with a high ceiling, empty except for the old-fashioned apparatus at the end, a relic of the days when water closets were first invented. The tank high on the wall was made of polished wood, mahogany perhaps, and leaked a little at the seams; a tuft of greenish moss grew on it here and there. The copper pipe that led down from it was covered with ver-digris. Her mother had explained that copper oxide formed a natural protective coating for the metal, and to polish it off would only mean that more verdigris formed to be polished off in its turn, until finally all the copper was consumed and the pipe would have to be replaced. Whether this was good science, it was the rule of the house, and the WC pipe was never polished. At the bottom of this pipe was the affair itself, consisting of the usual porcelain throne, stained here and there with rust and grayish splotches, and fitted with a seat of the same mahogany as the tank overhead, although, since people sat on the seat, it was worn and bare of varnish. A chain de-scended from the tank to the shoulder level of a seated person.

As it happened, there was also a skylight overhead, the only ventilation in this tall narrow room without windows, with its own chain to pull it open. One night years before, when she was only five or six, her father got up in the middle of the night to visit this room, and when he was finished he reached out in the dark and pulled the chain vigorously. But it was the chain of the skylight he took hold of, not that of the tank, and the whole contrivance, frame, glass, and hardware, came down from the ceiling with a deafening crash, awakening everyone in the building. Her father suffered only a slight cut on the forehead; the mass of the skylight missed him and struck the floor inches from his feet. Claire, outside the door, called anx-iously, "Paul, Paul, what is it?" Before he would allow anyone else to enter he carefully pulled the correct chain and waited until the apparatus had gone through its usual series of gar-gles and wheezes. Then he let them in. "This is an unsatisfac-tory arrangement," he said, examining the pear-shaped knob on the end of the skylight which was identical to that on the WC chain.

When the skylight was replaced her father specified that a different knob should be put on the end of the chain, and the workman found one in the Flea Market at the Porte de Clig-nancourt, near where he lived. It was a curious and attractive object, a brass lion's paw a little smaller than a human hand. But the workman, misunderstanding his instructions like all workmen, put it on the WC chain instead of the skylight chain. This led to the only joke that her father ever made, as far as Hermine could remember, although perhaps it wasn't a joke at all, only a euphemism that this shy and modest man found useful for referring to something he preferred not to speak of at all. Before leaving for the laboratory in the morning, his briefcase and umbrella ready, he would say, "Well, I must shake the hand of the lion," and disappear into the tall narrow room. Each family has its saying for these matters, kept secret from outsiders, and in the Savarin family it became "serrer la main au lion." This was shortened simply to "the lion." In a public place, a lecture hall or a train station, her mother would murmur, "Alors, Hermine, le lion," and Hermine would press her lips together in annoyance and go off obediently to the place in question. In England, she discovered, it was called the loo, and, clever bilinguist that she was, she quickly deciphered this as *le lieu*, the place. When with a certain pride she confided this discovery to her mother, Claire only turned away coldly without comment. She wasn't interested in comparative linguistics, her mind was mathematical rather than verbal, and in any case she believed these matters should be referred to as little as possible, and certainly not used as the subject of idle conversation.

Perhaps you don't see the point of all these private and intimate details of family life, or are offended by them. Or perhaps you wonder how I came into possession of these fact. How is it that I happen to be present in this private apartment in Rue François-Villon, occupied by people who are unusually secretive in their habits and suspicious of strangers, and even to penetrate the high narrow sanctum where the skylight crashed and the lion's paw came to be the daily companion of father, mother, and daughter? Well, any narrator is a magician, consider old Homer first of all, and how is it that Tolstoy (I've been reading him just recently) is able to tell us so accurately what Napoleon, who was a real person, was thinking on the eve of the Battle of Borodino? If you like, you may think of me as that small harmless two-winged insect of the family Muscidae, so popular as a metaphor for storytellers, envied by people who would like to be invisibly present in places where they shouldn't be; envied by all of us really, because we all have the same instincts, which is another way of saying that we are all storytellers, we all have the need to tell stories to others and ourselves in order to understand the point of our existence, and we all long, secretly and sometimes unconsciously, to be present and invisible when others are discussing their secrets, conducting their ablutions or excretions, copulating with forbidden partners, passing bribes to each other, cursing their fate aloud, counting out the suicide pills, or sharpening weapons for a crime. Perhaps you are more honest; you are excused from the general rule if you wish. But imagine this: imagine that you are in a room, let's say it's in the Palace of Versailles, and in the next room Marie Antionette is disrobing for her bath. There is a hole in the wall between the rooms, so small that, from the other side, no one could possibly see an eye fixed to it. Would you fix *your* eye to it? You wouldn't? Are you sure? Please don't be angry, I am only offering a hypothesis, in the spirit of pure science. And yet you are no better than God; and God is willing to watch Marie Antoinette disrobing for her bath, in fact it's part of His duties. How does He manage? I wonder why it has never occurred to anyone that God is perhaps not an old man with a white beard sitting on a cloud but only a fly on the wall.

Hermine (and I can tell you a lot about her), having done what she came into this sanctum to do, shook the hand of the lion, went out into the kitchen, and washed her hands in the sink, the only water tap in the apartment. The bathroom was down the passage, and to take a bath special arrangements had to be made with Mme Lacrosse, who then had to carry out various maneuvers to see that the water was heated and that the right valves were opened to enable it to mount to the second floor, and who had to be paid a franc for cleaning the tub afterward; and who, it should be added, saw very little reason for going to such a fuss about a human condition which was very natural, and would only repeat itself in a few days if the unwanted deposits were washed off; she herself never bothered (and who would pay her the franc for washing the tub?) and only grudgingly conceded to the custom on the part of her tenants. "Que voulez-vous, Mademoiselle? It's—" "Yes I know, Madame Lacrosse, it's the way of all flesh, but we don't all have to go that way." She herself, Hermine, bathed herself about once a week, if you insist on knowing, but the fly on the wall was not necessary in this case, for reasons I will get around to explaining in due time.

When she had washed her hands in the kitchen sink, Hermine changed her dress, slipping on a light-colored linen frock a little more frivolous than the black skirt she wore to the Sorbonne, added a cheap but fashionable hat from the Galeries Lafayette, took her purse and a shopping net hanging on the back of the kitchen door, and went out.

In the open-air market in Rue de la Convention she bought what she needed for the next few days: a bottle of milk, a little coffee in a twist of paper, potatoes, turnips, cheese, a baguette, a single egg, and a small jar of pâté as a special treat for her dinner. A pastry? No, that was unnecessary and expensive. She still felt herself to be the daughter of her mother, and this sense of austerity prevented her from falling into the most abandoned sorts of profligacy. If she denied herself the pastry, she thought, nothing very bad could happen to her. It was a kind of fence against her self-indulgence, making her stop *there* and go no further. If she didn't stop, what else might she buy? Chocolates? A bottle of brandy? Cigars? She smiled quite openly, ignoring the crowds around her in Rue de la Convention; when she was alone she often amused herself with her own thoughts and this was one of those times.

These things almost filled the shopping net, even though it would stretch to accommodate almost anything. She stopped finally, on impulse, at a small shop in Rue de Vaugirard that she had never entered before. It was most discreet, the windows were covered with white muslin, and if any of her neighbors should pass in the street, Mme Lacrosse for instance, they would hardly know she was in there. When she came out she had four or five more small packages in the net bag.

Back in the apartment she first put away the groceries and vegetables, set the pâté, the cheese, the milk, and the egg into the cooler with its damp burlap flap (there was no icebox in the apartment, another unnecessary luxury according to her mother), and then turned her attention to the packages from the parfumerie in Rue de Vaugirard.

The first one contained a kind of gilded oyster which she broke open to disclose a mirror, a little pad, and a quantity of rouge. She rubbed the pad in this and then touched it cautiously to her cheeks. She could see very little in the mirror inside the oyster, except a flash of alarming red. She turned to the kitchen mirror, which hung over the sink and was clouded over with gray patches so that it looked like a map of some unknown country. In it she made out her face with two red disks on it like a clown in a circus.

Flushing in her confusion, she got a cloth and soap and washed them off. It was really only necessary to be a little ashamed of oneself, she noticed, in order to have quite red cheeks. The next time she was more careful. She applied only a tiny dot of color to each cheek, then shut the gilded oyster and rubbed her cheeks vigorously with both hands. She stopped and examined her face in the mirror, and went on rubbing. When she had finished her cheeks glowed as though from the nip of a bright winter day. Whether this was owing to the color from the rouge, or from the rubbing itself, neither she nor anyone else could tell.

Now that she was more adept she knew how to use this same technique with the small pot of lip color and its brush. No one would have guessed that her lips were painted, imagining perhaps that she had bitten them to make them red, as the girls had done when she was at school with the Sisters, and been reprimanded for it. Another package did something for her eyes. She overdid this too the first time and had to wash it off. Finally she had it right, to the state where there was probably a touch of shadow around her eyes but no one could positively say so. Last came a flat jar of face powder; she wrapped a kitchen towel around her shoulders and throat and started to pat this on lightly. She thought perhaps she was doing the thing upside down and the powder should have gone on before the rouge, but it didn't seem to matter. When she shook out the towel it left a heady aroma floating in the air of the kitchen. Probably it would be gone before her mother came back from America.

Now she was arrayed in the way that the Sisters in school had assured her was the first step to damnation. She tried to make out the effect in the mirror, but she couldn't see much through the splotches. She bit her lip, became pensive for a moment, then went into her room and found her purse, a gray reticule with a silver clasp. She put on her hat and tied a gauze veil around it. Then she added a light velvet manteau, since it was November and the evening air was chill, and went out. Mme Lacrosse, that expert cynic, was not at all surprised to see her exiting at this time in the evening clad in all her finest; she only noted it.

Hermine got an omnibus in Rue de Vaugirard that took her to the Madeleine, and then set out on foot in the direction of Place Vendôme. It was a part of Paris she had been to only seldom and she had never dared to set foot in any of its shops, let alone its hotels. When she came to the Ritz, opposite the column with its statue of Napoleon in Roman robes, she strode in through the door which was ceremoniously opened for her by the doorman. The hall was a little daunting. Flunkies stood about in violet livery and white gloves. Plucking up her courage, she murmured a word to one of them. Without a trace of expression he inclined his head and pointed down a corridor to the right. Hermine was correctly if not elegantly dressed, and in the subdued light it was difficult to tell that her manteau and hat had come from the Galeries Lafayette and not from a shop in Rue St.-Honoré, even for so expert a critic as a chasseur at the Ritz. She went off down the corridor.

The lounge for ladies was a fairyland, an unimaginable paradise. Everything was onyx and marble and the fittings seemed to be solid gold. The electric light that came from panels in the ceiling was a soft apricot, a color highly flattering to the female complexion. At this time in the evening, the hour just before dinner, there were only a few other women in the lounge. The mirror covered an entire wall, behind the basins with their gold fittings. Hermine took off her veil, hat, and manteau, hung them on a hook behind her, and ran a comb briefly through her hair as her excuse for being in this place. Then, becoming very solemn, she studied her reflection in the glass.

As a child she had been thin and gawky, with large dark eyes and a swatch of black hair that resisted combing and stood up on her head in little tufts. Because of the poor mirror in the apartment, and the lack of any mirrors at all in the schools she went to, she had only an imperfect idea of how she had changed as she grew older. She grew up as most ugly duckings do, dreaming of another self. Then in her lycée class she encountered a poem of Baudelaire called "La vie antérieure," and she came to believe that she herself had had an Anterior Existence, a previous life more poetic and sensual than her present one, full of tropical imagery, populated with strange cats and pythons, enormous carnivorous flowers, in which she was an exotic feline like the others that twined through the jungle, lithe of limb, all-knowing and able to see in the dark, a creature of rare fancies and cruelties, driving others to animalesque excesses while remaining unscathed in her own innocence. What she saw now, to her own amused and slightly ironic surprise, was the exact fulfillment of that prophecy.

She was still thin, but her boniness had imperceptibly become the fine modeling that distinguishes classical beauty from the lumpy approximation that passes for it in nine out of ten women. Her gauntness had turned into a fashionable maigreur, with sharp cheekbones, a small firm chin, and a finely sculpted throat. Even her unruly hair, cut short like a boy's, coincided with the gamin look that was just coming into fashion. With her pale skin and dark expressive eyes she resembled the ermine after which her parents had unthinkingly named her.

She was still wearing the light linen frock in which she had gone to the market in Rue de la Convention. Unfortunately she couldn't see the rest of this creature from her former existence because it was concealed by the frock. She looked around her in the lounge. Two other women were busy at the mirror a little farther down, and a third had just come out of the gilded door of a stall and was making her way toward a wash-basin. Never would she have an opportunity like this. After a moment's hesitation she unbuttoned the frock and slipped it rapidly from her shoulders. Twisting her arms out of it, she pulled the ribbons of her shift from her shoulders and low-ered it as well. One of the women at the mirror, turning to see what she was doing, gasped and left the lounge abruptly. The other two paid her no attention. One of them, in fact, smiled at her distantly and then went back to her examination of her own face.

Hermine stared at a totally unknown creature, one she had never laid eyes on before, the headless animal she had con-cealed under her clothing for eighteen years. The upper part of her body was a demonstration of how boniness can be so attractive as to be positively painful. The vee of her throat met the clavicle exactly in the center of her chest. From this point the collarbones, as thin as flutes, angled outward to the points where they met the small knobs on the fronts of her shoul-ders. Continuing down her chest, the flat bone formed an av-enue with the shadows of the ribs visible on both sides of it. At symmetrical distances form it were two small hemispheres with conical tops, exactly resembling the apricots predicted by her complexion. They were so firm that there was no percep-tible line at the lower edge to distinguish them from the rest of her body; if they had been turned upside down they would have looked exactly the same. What were they for? They didn't seem to be utilitarian at all; they were the maddest sort of pure decoration, like Ming vases, pre-Attic kraters, or expen-sive crystal from Baccarat. They were not like flowers; they seemed artificial, exquisite, and very expensive. Hermine gazed on them with a totally satisfactory sense of possession.

Then she put her shift and frock back on, added the man-teau and hat, and left this opulent Etruscan chamber of waters, offering a smile to the white-gloved doorman as she passed out through the hall into the street. In a new Paris she was a new person. It was not only the vision of herself in the Ritz mirror that had transformed her outlook and converted the world from something strange to something familiar and valuable, a treasure that lay waiting for the twitch of her fingertips. The mirror had been only a catalyst, a messenger, a flicker in the retina that set off a mysterious process that had lain for some time latent in her glands. It had begun, she knew, with what had happened in that train from Victoria to Dover, as ludicrous as it had seemed at the time. Awakened by the heavy, somnolent, and (to give him the benefit of the doubt) all-unwitting hand of Professor Lancelot, her femininity expanded over the city like a breath of springtime, transforming her into that steely and stealthy feline of her Previous Existence and attracting other creatures helplessly to her by the sheer force of its invisible electricity. It was totally dark now and the gas lamps spread circles of pink onto Rue de la Paix. In between the lamps the pavement and the shops were dark as dreams, and full of interesting phantoms. Hermine passed from dark into light, and then the other way, as she strode along from lamp to lamp. She hadn't chosen to leave this way from Place Vendôme—the other way from the direction she had entered it—and yet she had. At the end of Rue de la Paix was the Boulevard des Capucines, and in the Boulevard des Capucines were cafés.

It may seem strange that a girl who was born in Paris and had lived there all her life had never set foot in a café in her own city, but such was the case. She had been to the café in Bougival on the Sunday excursions with her parents but never to one in Paris; it wasn't considered the proper thing for an unmarried girl. She finally selected the Café Américain, which was crowded and lively at this time of the evening. It was certainly grand enough, all red and gilt on the outside, with gilded chairs behind the hedge that separated them from the pavement. It was a little too cold to sit out on the terrasse, at least in her thin velvet cloak. She pushed open the door and entered.

Once inside it was a good deal easier than she thought. The

room was only about half full; most of the fashionable crowd was outside on the terrasse. A waiter waved a menu at a table and even flicked an invisible speck of dust off the chair with his napkin. She was seated and examining a menu describing a complexity of gustatory sensualism that seemed likely to bewilder her completely. "Coffee," she said firmly.

"Grand ou petit?"

"Petit."

When the coffee came it was in fact very small. At home in Rue François-Villon it would have been regarded as something for a dolls' tea party. Under it was a saucer with the number 75 on it. This was evidently what the coffee cost. Well, that wasn't too much. (She was sure it was seventy-five centimes and not francs, enough to buy a horse or a sofa.) She thought she had about seven francs in her purse. She looked around at the other patrons. Most of them were couples or foursomes. Only a few had come alone: florid women in flamboyant dresses and feathered hats, some of them carrying parasols even though it was pitch dark outside now, and young gentlemen in evening dress who fingered their mustaches while they covertly examined these ladies. One such woman, in a red dress with ostrich feathers at the neck, had tired of waiting and was delicately eating a Fraise Herma. A pair of couples, elegant young people who were evidently on their way to the theater, were having vermouths with lemon. A waiter pushing a pastry cart down through the rows of tables passed directly by her. She stopped him.

After some consideration she selected a tarte aux fraises, which looked exquisite enough that one might murder for it. The saucer under it said 3.50. All well still, provided there was really seven francs in her purse. A tip for the waiter! How much was needed? She had no idea. All at once she was in a panic.

To recover from it she began eating the strawberry tart with the small silver spoon provided. She was after all still only a child, or she had been until a half-hour before, when she had bloomed all at once into a woman before the mirror in the Ritz Hotel, and she ate every scrap of it with the depraved and mindless sensualism of the young.

GLOWSTONE

When she had finished the last crumb and drunk her coffee she looked around the café again. It was in the shape of a blocky letter U with the pantry and kitchens in the middle. On her side it was a narrow room with imitation marble columns and a pressed-tin ceiling in an elaborate embossed design. The lamps that hung from the ceiling, small moonlike spheres the size of lemons, provided only subdued illumination. The tables were wire with imitation-marble tops.

She began studying the other patrons more carefully than she had at first. At the next table was a man of sixty with his top hat upside down on the chair next to him and his gloves in it; his companion was a young woman her own age. She tried to decide whether they were a businessman and his mistress or a father and daughter—was there a family resemblance?—or perhaps only a young lady who had happened to encounter a friend of her family in the street and been invited for a coffee. This question was settled when she heard the young woman say, through a silence that fell for a moment over the room, "I should be enchanted of course if you should ask me." Farther on were four young men she took for stockbrokers or young bankers; they were all dressed conservatively and drinking bocks, wiping their mustaches carefully afterwards with their knuckles. She told herself a story about them too. When they finished the bocks they would go around for four seamstresses they knew who lived in Levallois-Perret beyond the freightyards; they would take them out to dinner at a brasserie and then they would all go off to the Folies-Bergères. Afterward—Hermine didn't know very much about the afterwards in such affairs. In any case this game of telling stories about total strangers was fascinating. She went on to examine a couple, a gaunt solemn frowning young woman whose head was concealed under a shawl and a dark man with a stubble of beard on his cheeks, and decided she was a nun who had stolen out of a convent to rendezvous with an unfrocked priest. After the café, they would go for a walk in the Champs-Élysées, four feet apart and not daring to touch, and at the end of the evening she would throw herself into the Seine.

Beyond this unhappy clerical pair was a handsome olive-skinned young man in a black suit, a white shirt, and a necktie with fine gold stripes. With him was a large young woman with an elongated craggy face, as though it were inexpertly carved out of granite, and her hair done in a bun like a brioche. Her hands seemed to belong to somebody else, a male even larger than she was. She seemed nervous and scouted constantly around the room like a searchlight. Setting her story-telling instinct to work, Hermine tested the hypothesis that they were an English heiress and a young Italian hairdresser who hoped to marry her for her money. Then she recognized them. They were Carlo Bini and Délicienne Maedl, the two assistants from the laboratory.

Hermine was startled. She had seen them a dozen or so times when she had gone with her mother to the Institute, and even exchanged a word or two with them, but it was dislocating to see them here. In the laboratory they wore stained white smocks; now they were dressed in a kind of pretentious and plebeian imitation of fashionable clothing. Bini had set his bowler on the table with his gloves in it, and she was in a mauve dress with purple ribbons. It wasn't that there was anything wrong about Bini and Mlle Maedl going to a café; after all they were both of age and free to live what lives they wanted. It was that this handsome young Italian and this Swiss spinster belonged to the world of the laboratory, and Hermine was unable for the moment to attribute to them any other existence, in the way that a very young child believes that his teacher lives and sleeps in the school and is in some way a part of the school furniture, and is aghast and shocked, when he is out with his mother, to see her shopping for eggplants in the market. The fact that they were together, and had therefore achieved at least some kind of intimacy that was not scientific, was a lesser surprise.

This shock lasted only for an instant and was succeeded by a quick resourcefulness. Bini saw her mother every day and it would not do to have it reported that she went to cafés on the Grands Boulevards after dark. Reaching into her reticule, she took out six francs and set them on the saucer where the pastry had been. Three francs fifty and seventy-five centimes, she believed, came to something over four francs, and the rest of it, whatever that amounted to, was surely an adequate tip. Then she took her reticule, got up smoothly from the table, and left the café, keeping her eyes fixed on the right, away from Bini and Mlle Maedl, on the pretext of looking at something very interesting in exactly that direction. The waiter, sweeping up the coins, sized her up for exactly what she was: a girl who had never been to a café before and left far too much for the waiter.

She got home safely, observed only by Mme Lacrosse from her loge, and let herself into the apartment with a little flush in her cheeks. She was pleased with herself and confident that Mme Lacrosse, who was garrulous but never passed on gossip, would say nothing about her having gone out at night and with rouge on her cheeks (but she would hardly have noticed this). In the days that followed Hermine reveled in her new-found freedom and constantly discovered new ways to take advantage of it. When her mother was home she had taken omnibuses only to places where she had some reason to go, to school or to some errand to the stores. Now she rode these lumbering and capacious vehicles all over Paris; she learned all the lines, knew the fares by heart, and got on terms of friendship with the conductors. In fine weather the best place to ride was on top, à l'impériale as it was called. At the rear of the omnibus there was a fine curved stairway so that ladies could mount to the upper deck, and so that a gentleman following after her, one day, caught a glimpse of ankle (she had bought herself a pair of smoke-colored silk stockings at the Bon Marché) and attempted to engage her in conversation. What do you think, Mademoiselle, about these new department stores they're building now? And which do you think is nicer, the Belle Jardinière or the Samaritaine? She smiled, said little, and looked away in the opposite direction at the passing shops and the smart dresses of the women in Rue de Rivoli; but she was pleased with herself.

She went to a hundred places she had never been before:

the Musée Carnavalet, the shops in Rue St.-Honoré, the quaint and exquisite old Place des Vosges, the Canal St.-Martin with its barges and its boisterous lower-class children. One morning she went to the Halles, where she wandered like a wayward child in a fairy tale among the porters staggering along under baskets of vegetables or meat, fishwives shrieking their wares, boys on tricycles laden with bread threading their way through the crowds, enormous wagons backing up to discharge their loads amid the cracking of whips and the heavy oaths of the drivers, the nostrils of the Percherons exuding steam in the crisp morning air. To tell the truth, this was a morning when she should have been at a lecture. She came back with a single egg *(Mademoiselle wants a single egg? Very well, all our other eggs are married but here is a single egg for you,* shouted the melon-breasted vendeuse), wrapped in a cone of newspaper with a loop so she could carry it on her finger, her excuse to herself for having gone to such a dubious and unsavory part of Paris alone.

She had almost forgotten now about her other escapade, her visit to the café on the Boulevard des Capucines, but she wasn't to escape from the consequences of her rash act so easily. As she came back from the Halles that morning with her egg she found a pneumatique stuck into her door, a message of the kind called by Parisians a petit bleu, propelled through a tube under the city by a vacuum apparatus. She had never received one before and neither had her parents as far as she knew; you could send a letter for a tenth of the price and it got there the next day. Opening it, she found an invitation from Carlo Bini to go to dinner, "during absence," the telegraphic style explained, "your mother from Paris." And it concluded, "Reply pneumatically," a strange term that was evidently the result of the rule that one paid by words; Bini, like most people, did not have unlimited money.

She hesitated only for a few moments. That there was an element of the dubious in the message she could not doubt. The phrase "during absence" referred, evidently, not only to her mother's absence from Paris but to her own behavior during this absence. She knew now that he had seen her at the Café Américain. If she and Bini were friends, she read between the lines, her going to the café alone would have no consequences, that is her mother would never find out about it. In short a polite form of blackmail. Was it then such a terrible crime to go to a café in the Boulevard des Capucines, was one to be burnt at the stake for it like Joan of Arc?

However dining with Bini was by no means as unpleasant an idea as being burnt at the stake. He was a strikingly handsome young man, and as for his power of knowledge over her, she knew something about him too, that he had an inexplicable interest in the totally unattractive Mlle Maedl. Perhaps he imagined that, although he had seen her, she had not seen him in the café. And it was true her mother was out of the city; who knew when such an opportunity would happen again? She smiled, became thoughtful, went to the post office in Rue de Vaugirard, and sent her own petit bleu, which contained only three words, "It depends where."

Because she had no intention of allowing herself to be taken by Bini or anyone else to a resort of doubtful reputation, which meant for practical purposes a restaurant anywhere near the Grands Boulevards or the Butte Montmartre. She had taken enough chances already by putting on cosmetics, demi-disrobing in the Hotel Ritz, and then going off to eat a strawberry tart in the Boulevard des Capucines.

Bini came at seven, approaching along the sidewalk while she watched him covertly from the window. He was dressed as he had been at the café, in a dark suit, a white shirt, and a necktie in gold stripes, and as he turned into the doorway he took off his bowler and held it respectfully in his hand. Through the silent house she heard him announcing to Mme Lacrosse, "I present myself for Mademoiselle Savarin."

"Oh, là là. Well, present yourself upstairs. There's no bell and I'm not going to walk upstairs for every Johnny who comes with a chapeau-melon."

Hermine had put on rouge and a light touch of powder again. Flushed from this, or from a slightly panicked sense of escapade, she crossed quickly to the door and opened it before he knocked. "Good evening, Monsieur Bini. That seems silly. Shall I call you Carlo? Please wait outside. I'll be out in just a minute."

She shut the door in his face, slipped on her manteau, and went to put on her hat before the mirror in the kitchen, adding the gauze veil which she tied under her chin. As she gave the mirror a last quick look it seemed to her that her lips were pale and dull like a child's. She bit them hard, first the upper and then the lower. She wondered if anyone had ever died of blood poisoning from this trick. Probably it wasn't possible to poison yourself by biting your lips. Then she went to the door, opened it, and slipped out quickly onto the landing before he had a chance to come in.

"And may I call you Hermine?" he asked, having had time to collect his wits on this subject.

"Please do. What a lovely evening. And how nice of you to ask me. I so seldom dine en ville these days when Maman is away." (She had never been in a restaurant in her life without her parents.) "And since my return from England" (a good touch; Bini had never been to England) "life has been so dull. Although I have been *terribly* occupied with my studies at the Sorbonne."

She was babbling. They stole out rather furtively past the Medusa-figure of Mme Lacrosse planted on the chair by her little window. In the street Carlo put his hat back on. She saw now that in addition to the bowler he was actually carrying a rolled umbrella like an Englishman, and also that there was a diamond stickpin in his tie. At least it pretended to be a diamond; probably it was only from the Bon Marché like her stockings.

He said, "There's a cab stand just at the corner."

"Oh I never go in a cab. The omnibus will take us to the Luxembourg, and from there it's only a step to the restaurant."

"The restaurant?" He gazed at her curiously.

"Yes, the Bouillon Duval in Boulevard St.-Michel. I used to go often to Duval's with my parents. After Papa's death we haven't gone out as much. The food is good there and it's not expensive. I don't know if your necktie will be suitable. It's a family sort of restaurant. Anyhow," she concluded, "that's where we're going."

A family sort of restaurant was probably not what Carlo had in mind. He himself had dined at Duval's many times when he was short of cash at the end of the month. He capitulated to her formidable will. After all, it wouldn't be a good idea to start the evening with a quarrel. They got off the omnibus at the Luxembourg, walked through the gardens just before the gates were closed by the keepers, and found themselves on the Boul' Mich' in the middle of a crowd of students, artists, and Left Bank bohemians, some of them a little raucous. Hermine was unperturbed. She strode along blithely, pushing her way through knots of people who stood blocking the pavement. When they came to the restaurant he opened the door for her and they entered together.

The place was crowded but they found a table. The waitresses were soberly garbed women who looked something like Sisters of Charity. It was certainly true that it was not expensive. They had soup, fish, boiled beef, vegetables, bread and cheese, with a miniature carafe of wine for Carlo and a cup of tilleul for Hermine, all for five francs. It was less than she had paid for her coffee and pastry at the Café Américain, if you included her enormous tip. The only trouble was that there was no place for Carlo's hat, umbrella, and gloves; the table was tiny and it only had two chairs. He stood the umbrella against the wall, put his gloves in his pocket, and after some thought ate with his hat on; several other people were doing the same.

Hermine could scarcely contain her delight at his predicament. She made an intense effort to conceal her smile, an adult skill and one she wasn't used to. She would have to learn it, since she expected that she was going to find many more things amusing in this wide world that was just opening up to her.

* * *

Outside in the Boul' Mich' again the crowds were even thicker. It was like pushing your way through a Brazilian jungle to make your way down the sidewalk. Carlo was saying something to her.

"What?"

"A cup of coffee?"

She nodded, since the buzz from the crowd made it difficult to speak. Before she knew what had happened he had found a cab standing at the curb and pushed her into it, following after her into the dark furry interior, as it were the inside of an insect. She opened her mouth to say something, wondered if she ought to force her way past him out of the cab, and changed her mind. Evidently Carlo had murmured a word to the cabman as he got in, because the man snapped his whip at his horse and the cab moved off rapidly through the traffic. She was a little indignant. She sat crowded as far as she could into her side of the cab and remained silent. As a matter of fact Carlo was a perfect gentleman during the trip, sitting as silently as she and holding his umbrella between his knees. The cab spun along at a trotting pace across the river and came out onto the Right Bank. At Châtelet it turned onto Rue de Rivoli and then turned again into Avenue de l'Opéra. It was headed directly toward the cafés on the Grands Boulevards.

"Monsieur Bini—"

"You were going to call me Carlo."

"That was before you kidnapped me and brought me to this part of Paris where I don't care to go."

"Oh bah!" He laughed. "We're only going to have a coffee. If you like we can go back and have it on the Boul' Mich'. With all those unwashed artists."

"Oh no. Since you've seen fit to arrange matters in this way." She found it difficult to sort out her own emotions. They were, first of all, indignation at this high-handed way he was treating her. Second, a pleasure that they were going to an interesting part of Paris that was ordinarily denied to her; and third a dark and quite sensual fascination at the thought of being stolen by a man against her will in a darkened cab. This last feeling she was not really responsible for, and indeed we are not responsible for any of our feelings, only for our acts. So Hermine had read at least in a novel by Benjamin Constant.

When the cab stopped in front of the Café Américain her thoughts worked rapidly again. She felt a renewed indignation that, of all the cafés he might have brought her to, he had brought her to the embarrassing one where he had seen her just two nights before. But perhaps it was the only café he knew; after all he wasn't rich and probably came to the Grands Boulevards only on special occasions. Did he have the same scheme in mind for her that he had for Mlle Maedl? She wasn't sure what this was but she disapproved of it. She stepped delicately out of the cab onto the pavement.

When they were seated he studied the menu with a frown but she left hers lying on the table.

"A tarte aux fraises."

A cat-and-mouse smile appeared on his lips. "Do you come here often?"

"Very seldom."

They fell into a truce, which continued after the waiter had taken their orders. She had never been here before, in any case she had not seen him here, and for his part he had not seen her. Maman would never know about any of this. And what had she done that was so shameful? She had simply gone to a café. She was ready to tell her mother about this herself. (She wasn't, but so she pretended.) His part of the secret, of course, was that he had appeared in public, under conditions of obvious intimacy, with the unpalatable Délicienne Maedl, which marked him either as a cynical sensualist with no standards at all or as a man hopelessly desperate for any female companionship. "And do you come here often with the ladies?" she asked him with the slight touch of malice that came so easily to her.

"Hardly."

"But obviously you've been here before. And hardly anyone," she pointed out, looking around the room, "comes here alone." As they could both see, the only solo patrons were the dubious women and the young men in the evening dress looking them over.

"What can you know about such things? You speak so oddly, Hermine. I'm not sure I understand you."

"I'd be surprised if you did. I hardly understand myself. I don't think anyone understands anyone. I certainly don't understand you. On the other hand I do, quite well."

"You're a very strange girl."

When they had finished their coffee and pastries—he had an éclair, she the strawberry tart—she slipped her cloak around her shoulders and they went out onto the boulevard. This time she made no objection to being handed into a cab. She was a little startled, however, to hear him tell the cabman to drive to the Bois instead of the address in Rue François-Villon.

"I have to be up early for a lecture."

"Oh, so do I," he agreed. "I'm at the laboratory at eight o'clock every morning."

"Oh, the laboratory." Dutifully, like a well-brought-up young lady, she plied him with questions about himself. "Tell me about your work in the laboratory."

He sighed. "Ah, my work in the laboratory." It was not really what he had intended to talk about in the cab. "But you know, Hermine, in the end any job becomes routine, even when it's dedicated to high causes, even when one works at the Savarin Institute at the side of your mother, advancing human knowledge and alleviating the sufferings of mankind." Hermine had heard all this so often! "In the end," he went on, "what we do consists of the endless refining of ore samples. That and the measurement of the emanations, which we all know by heart. Day after day we read the scale of the electroscope and record the results in our laboratory logs, endless sheets of paper covered with figures. My fingers bleed from the effects of glowstone"—he held them up to show her but they were invisible in the darkness—"and I fall into gloomy thoughts. Sometimes, Hermine, our work at the Institute pales into insignificance compared to the deeper human problems."

"Human problems?"

"Loneliness, isolation, companionship. The profoundness of the night. The need for love."

"There's a need for science too. I supposed there would be others to satisfy the need for love. Those women in the café."

He was struck dumb by this and gazed at her in puzzlement. After a moment he said, "I hardly think you know what you are talking about."

"No, I don't, really. Do you? Rambling on about companionship and the profoundness of the night."

"I think I do." There was another silence, and then he said, "The other day I was looking through a book on astronomy. It explained the exact shape of the shadow that extends out from the earth into space. There are two shadows, in fact. Both are conical in shape. The umbra is black as pitch. The penumbra, extending tens of thousands of miles into space, is an indeterminate gray. Only when there is an eclipse of the moon are we aware of these two gulfs of darkness. But they are always there. We think of space as empty and luminous, filled with the light of the sun. But the shadow of the earth extends always out into the void. That frightens one. The eternal silence of those vast spaces that surround us."

"I believe you're quoting Pascal."

"Where did you learn that?"

"In the lycée."

"For a mere girl you're very learned. Pascal also says," he went on, "that man is only a reed, yet he is a thinking reed. It doesn't take much to destroy him. A drop of water, a current of air. And when he is gone, those eternal spaces are still there. The black cone of shadow still sweeps on endlessly through them."

The cab had entered the Bois. It was even darker than the city; only a few lights twinkled here and there from a refreshment kiosk or a restaurant half-hidden in the woods.

"It's almost as dark here as in the earth's penumbra."

"We are in the earth's penumbra, Hermine. It's not just a figure of speech. Here at night in Paris, we stand at its base. From us it extends out into the void. That is what night means."

"But after night comes day. And then night, and then day again."

"Yes. For a while. But in time the earth will cool, and become only a lifeless stone circling the sun."

He was silent, brooding over this, or thinking of the next part of his speech. She waited patiently for him to go on. When he did, it was in a vein of light melancholy rather than Pascalian profondeur.

"But you are right. Morning always comes. Morning in Paris. I used to dream of that when I was a student in Bologna, where it always seemed to be evening. And then I came here. And in fact, Paris in the morning is something exquisite and unique, a thing found nowhere else in the world. It is like a young girl. A promise of freshness, of renewal. Of restored virginity."

Against the window she could see the outline of his head rimmed in starlight. He took her hand.

"Do you know, Hermine, I respect you enormously. I have known you for—how many years? A good many—since you were a child. But I knew you *only* as a child, the child of your mother, another person I respect more than anything on earth. And yet you always held a special place in my thoughts. As I watched you grow older, you became a kind of vision for me, a vision of Paris." He corrected himself slightly; his French was precise, with only a light Italian accent. "An image of Paris. It's called the City of Light. And you seemed to me a creature of light, a charming sprite, a child innocent as the morning. And then all at once I noticed one day that you were no longer a child."

"It coincided with a time when my mother was out of Paris."

He seemed not to hear her. He turned to her urgently, and his hand left hers and slipped, as though unconsciously, to the skirt that covered her knees. "There is light in the world and there is darkness. The darkness terrifies me. And for me, you are light."

She dislodged the hand. "You know, everybody tells me they respect me enormously, and everybody puts his hand on my leg. What is that up ahead?"

"The Lac Inférieur."

"Why is it inferior?"

He sighed. "It's not inferior, it's just lower than the Lac Supérieur. You can go boating there. Why won't you respect me, Hermine, as I respect you?"

"I respect you enormously. For that reason, I wouldn't dream of laying a hand on you. An eminent scientist! A colleague of my mother in the Institute! It would be unthinkable. Do you know I've never been to the Bois de Boulogne?"

"Well, you've been to it now."

"Oh, I don't call this going to the Bois. This is only seeing it from a cab."

The cabman, crossing the bridge between the two lakes, turned his vehicle around with a snap of the whip and headed it back toward the Champs-Élysées.

"Where are you going, you idiot?" shouted Carlo in vexation. "Around the lake once more!"

"I absolutely must go home now," she told him. "It's after eleven. If you won't tell the cab to take me back, I'll walk. Now wouldn't that be ludicrous."

"To Rue François-Villon," sighed Carlo to the square back visible in the darkness.

Alone in the empty apartment, placidly fixing her breakfast, Hermine finally worked out what this "enormous respect" amounted to. She was Hermine, her mother was Claire, and Claire was the director of the Institute. Therefore if Carlo married Hermine, he would become the son-in-law of the Institute, so to speak, and in a good position to succeed Madame when she retired. But he had left Lancelot out of his calculations. Lancelot was a good deal younger than her mother, and would no doubt assume the mantle of authority when it dropped from her own shoulders. But Carlo had the optimism of youth, and of his own handsomeness. As for his discourses on Pascalian anxiety, they were only part of his fine Italian technique of courtship. What it came to in the end was that she ought to give herself to him because he was afraid of the dark. And yet, and yet, she thought, meditating further, perhaps he was sincere. Child that he was—it was he who was the child, not she—he quite possibly believed everything he said. Perhaps all the activities of men, from the Neanderthal dragging home a bison to his mate to the most exquisite and specialized discoveries of the modern scientist, were in the end only an impulse to impress the female, to win her favors. Everybody said it was love that made the world go round, it was in all the songs. Now she saw abruptly and brilliantly what this meant. She didn't distinguish in her mind between love and sex, and besides it wasn't possible in French; there was only the word amour. Of course, there was "enormous respect." She smiled like Mona Lisa, remembering Professor Lancelot's nodding eroticism in the train and Carlo's earnestness as he discoursed of shadows and void and groped for her skirt in the darkness.

Finishing her coffee and brioche, she went to the kitchen sink and washed her face thoroughly, removing any possible trace of the cosmetics of the night before. Then she went off to her lecture at the Sorbonne.

The next time Carlo came for her it was on a Sunday afternoon, and in an open victoria instead of a cab. He too was transformed; he was in a blue singlet with a light linen jacket over it, a pair of linen trousers, and a straw boater, and he had with him a wicker picnic basket.

It was a sparkling day in late autumn. The carriage went along the Rue de la Convention and crossed the river on the Pont Mirabeau. Threading its way through Auteuil, it entered the Bois just by the racecourse and clip-clopped on down the avenue, thronging with promenaders and ladies with parasols, toward the two lakes. Following Carlo's directions, it stopped at a spot not far from the lakes where a circle of trees concealed a patch of grass just large enough for a picnic. He seemed to give the carriage driver a great deal of money; the ghost of a wince passed over his face as the banknotes slipped from his hand. When we go back, she thought, I'll suggest that we take the omnibus.

She stood waiting until he had opened the basket and un-
furled a white linen cloth on the grass. Then she knelt to help
him with the rest. There were boiled eggs, a roast chicken,
rolls, wine, and a bottle of lemonade for Hermine in case she
didn't care for wine. Where he had come by all these things
was not clear. Perhaps from a charcuterie or the restaurant of
some hotel. She thought of asking him, "Do you often take
ladies to picnic in the Bois?" but decided she had teased him
enough. He was a charming person really, he couldn't be more
correct and polite, and he was very handsome.

People coming along the footpath a few yards away turned
to look at them through the trees. They were a pretty picture:
the white cloth gleaming on the grass, the rustic basket, Carlo
disguised as a young artist from the Latin Quarter, a Rodolfo
escaped from the opera, and Hermine in a girlish white frock
with pink ribbons in the sleeves and skirt. She had had the
dress since she was a girl of fourteen but she was still the same
size. Her appetite was that of a child too; she ate two-thirds of
the chicken and all the boiled eggs, and then discovered a pair
of cream buns in a bag at the bottom of the basket. She ate
one and put the other away, hoping Carlo wouldn't have the
appetite for it. She declined the wine in favor of the lemonade. He nibbled at a drumstick, looking at her thoughtfully.

When they finished their meal and folded up the linen cloth
they went off toward the lake, Carlo carrying the basket and
Hermine her reticule with the silver clasp. At the boathouse
Carlo, getting out more money, rented a long elegant rowboat
painted white with blue gunwales and seats. The attendant
handed her into it; she felt something like Marie Antoinette
on the pond at Versailles. When her mother came back, of
course, it would be off to the guillotine. Carlo sprang in lightly
with the basket and grasped the oars with a capable air. She
had never been in a boat before and was told where to sit, at
the very back, where she could trail one hand through the
greenish lucid water. Carlo sat in the middle facing her (although she had often seen boats from the shore, it had never
quite struck her that one rowed them facing backwards) with
another seat between them.

"How do you tell where you are going?"

"Eyes in the back of my head, and discreet glances from time to time."

"Be careful, Carlo."

"Don't worry, I'm an experienced boatman."

"Are there boats in Bologna?"

"No, that's Venice. I learned to row here in the Bois."

"With other ladies?" She couldn't help herself.

"Don't joke. I'm a serious person. I don't go boating with just anyone."

With great effort, she managed not to ask him if he had gone boating with Délicienne Maedl. Officially, she didn't know that he had the slightest interest in Mlle Maedl.

"Your hat," she told him, "is called a boater in English."

"In French, a canotier."

"I know. But this isn't a canoe."

"Canoes are very unstable. I wouldn't dream of taking a girl out in a canoe. Not one that I respected."

"Ah, your enormous respect."

This seemed to remind him of something and he stopped rowing. From his gestures—she could almost read his mind—it was evident that he was about to take off his jacket. It was an exceptionally mild day for November, still it was hardly warm enough for a man to take off his jacket. He pretended to sweat. Removing his boater, he mopped his absolutely dry brow. Then he unbuttoned the jacket, took it off, and folded it carefully, laying it on the seat of the boat beside the hat. Now he looked even more like someone in a picture by Manet. The duck-egg-blue singlet exposed his shoulders and his strong young neck. He resumed rowing, and the reason for his removing his jacket became apparent. With each stroke, as he leaned back on the seat and forced his muscles into play, his curving pectorals swelled in an impressive display of manliness, so prominent they seemed almost deformed. They reminded her of the secondary sexual characteristics of certain animals she had learned about in her biology class: the swollen red wattles of turkeys, the tails of peacocks, the green behinds of baboons. His biceps were likewise well developed, standing like apples on his arms. It was not clear how in his sedentary job he had become so muscular, but what was clear was that he wished her to notice these things. Just as she had been expected, like a well-brought-up young lady, to inquire about his work at the laboratory, now she was expected to take an interest in his muscles. She became mischievous, her besetting vice.

"Your arms are so strong. Could I feel them?"

"Feel them?"

He became grave, and a little twitch appeared at the corner of his mouth as though a fly had settled there. He laid down the oars and bent forward, kneeling on the seat between them. She too leaned forward from her seat and squeezed the distended muscle as he flexed the arm. When a man offers his muscle to be felt, he puts his arm into a very primitive position, raised high with the fingers clenched, as though he were about to smite somebody with a stone ax.

"I think you have hidden in there a couple of the hardboiled eggs from the lunch basket."

"Hermine." He bent forward a little farther and set his fingers softly on her cheek. Her smile became uncertain and furtive. She bent her head to the side, but the hand followed. The next thing she knew his lips were on her mouth; she felt the cleft between them and their warm moist insistence. He lunged forward, she swerved to one side, and the boat tipped alarmingly. The gunwale went under and a splash of water poured into it. She made a little cry. His boater and linen jacket slid from the seat into the bottom of the boat, where an inch of dirty water now sloshed back and forth.

He fished out the dripping hat and jacket and she composed herself. "Carlo," she told him, "you respect me so enormously that if you are not careful you are going to drown us both."

When they came back to Rue François-Villon—in the omnibus, not a cab, and Carlo carrying his damp hat and jacket in one hand and the picnic basket in the other—he set down his burdens and attempted to kiss her hand in full view of Mme Lacrosse. It was a harmless enough gesture, in a way an apology for his rampage in the boat, and ordinarily Hermine might have accepted it with tolerant amusement. Still it was a liberty and one she was not sure she ought to permit him, at least not in the view of the old woman framed in the window of her loge. When he took her hand she felt the roughness of his fingers from the scars of the laboratory. A flash of repugnance came over her, and for an instant she saw the statue by the Médicis fountain in the Luxembourg, the shadow of the monster Polyphemus lurking over the unwitting lovers. She pulled her hand away. He seemed disappointed, but attributed it no doubt to the presence of the concièrge. "Hermine—"

"Goodbye!" She fled up the stairs. "And thank you for the—" She reached the landing and slipped in through the door of the apartment before she finished the sentence. But once inside she hurried through to her bedroom and pushed open the shutters of the window. He was still standing on the pavement, uncertain whether to wait for an omnibus or start walking back to his own lodgings on the other side of the Sorbonne.

"Au revoir, Carlo!"

He looked up and found the source of the voice. "Au revoir?" he repeated hopefully. "Then I'll see you again?"

"You can see me again and again and again, here in the window. Like a novio in Spain." She burst into peals of laughter and closed the shutters.

Later she had second thoughts. Her hilarity was really hysterical and had little to do with the incidents of the day, as humorous as some of them had been. It was a symptom of stress, indecision, and a badly overloaded nervous symptom. She spent the next two days the prey of mixed emotions, so complicated that she herself could hardly sort them out. Fear and awe, first, of her mother's authority, made more tremendous now by the Sophoclean tragedy of her widowhood. A mischievous delight in the things she had got away with while her mother was gone. A swelling womanly satisfaction that she was now on a par with her mother and other women, not merely a daughter, a child. A lurking curiosity about what her mother would do when she returned, and a perplexity as to what to tell her about Carlo, or whether she should tell her anything at all. Although she had never been intimate with her mother, she had always been truthful with her, since up to now there had never been anything to conceal. How could she explain her bizarre behavior, which seemed strange even to her, to the mother who had disapproved so strongly of her going punting on the Thames with three students? It wasn't a question now of punting with three students but of going alone to a café on the Grands Boulevards, of dining tête-à-tête with Carlo, of roaming around Paris with him in a darkened cab, of picnicking with him in the Bois, and of being kissed violently if ineffectually in a boat. She began to anticipate her mother's return with a kind of terror. In her dreams, which persisted into her waking hours, she saw the gaunt black-clad shape getting out of the cab and passing with dignity into the house, stopping no doubt at the loge to have a friendly word with Mme Lacrosse, and then coming up the stairs to confront her with her misdeeds; a remote, marmoreal, and accusing figure, whose sanctity now bore the even greater authority of her grief. It would have been far better, thought Hermine, if she had gone to stay with her aunt in Place des Victoires. Yet if she had done that, all these things which still tingled like Christmas ornaments in her mind would not have happened. Was there still a faint odor of face powder lingering in the kitchen? Before her mother came back, Hermine threw away the small boxes from the parfumerie.

On the Tuesday after the picnic in the Bois she heard a sound in the street below. She went to the window and opened it. Just as she had expected, a cab was standing in the street and her mother was being handed down by the cabman. On the other side of the cab there stepped down a tall man clad in white, with a resolute jaw and iron-blue eyes. He wore a broad-brimmed white hat, and the hair over his ears was silver. Her mother was clad in her usual black dress, but she had a rosebud pinned to the bodice and she was carrying a small dog under one arm. The tall man in white seized her baggage from the cabman and carried it to the door without effort. After he set the bags down he took off his hat, revealing an alabaster brow which contrasted strongly with the chapped brown of his cheeks. He bent, seized her mother's hand, and touched it to his lips.

The bags were carried into the house; Hermine heard them bumping in the passage. In all this bustle Claire almost forgot the leaden case with its tiny vial of glowstone. In another moment the cab would have driven off with it. Clapping her hand to her mouth in amused dismay, she went back to get it.

V

Upon her return to Paris from America, Claire threw herself into the work of the Institute with a renewed energy and dedication. The isolation of pure glowstone was achieved now and the staff of the laboratory went on to other tasks, including the effects of glowstone emanations on plants and animals.

Claire herself took charge of this new branch of the research, with Carlo Bini as her assistant. Milkweed and cow parsley were to be grown in a greenhouse and subjected to the emanations of glowstone for measured periods. The first rats appeared in the laboratory, some of them with artificially induced tumors or infected with malaria. Claire and Bini carefully monitored the effects of the emanations on these subjects, and compared them with another population of identical rats who were not treated with glowstone.

Another branch of the research, under Lancelot, concentrated on industrial and commercial uses for glowstone. Luminescent paint had already been developed several years before, while Paul was still alive, and was used in the manufacture of watch faces and compass dials. Glowstone lent an attractive mauve or violet hue to glass, and wineglasses tinted by this process had been produced by a factory at Lagny-sur-Marne. The possibility of luminescent advertising signs or stage sets for theaters was also under consideration.

Meanwhile the drudge work of the laboratory, the task of refining the Stockhausen earth into concentrated salts and then into pure glowstone, went on. For the most part this was done by Onyx Fabre and Délicienne Maedl, with the help of a small corps of students from the Sorbonne who came and went and were more or less interchangeable. Hermine was not one of these; she had never expressed any desire to work in the Institute and Claire preferred not to have her, for reasons she herself couldn't quite put her finger on. The child wasn't serious, that was one way of putting it; but another way was that she had the air of knowing too much, and that was just the opposite. In addition to her guilt at having left the work of the Institute for so long on her jaunt to America, Claire felt another guilt which was really only an appendix of the same emotion: that Hermine had seen her come back from America accompanied by Blanco, wearing a rose and carrying a lapdog, and that she had allowed Blanco to kiss her hand. How had that happened exactly? She certainly hadn't planned to have it happen, or anticipated it. Blanco had a way of causing things to happen in spite of the will of any other persons involved. He gave the effect sometimes not of a mortal being but of a Primary Causative Agent, a kind of good-natured Zeus who compelled clouds and chose mortals at will for his amorous intentions. His presence in Paris, and his declared admiration for her, troubled her a little when she thought about it from time to time. However, he didn't make a nuisance of himself. He called at the house once or twice, and invited her to dinner which she declined. He was constantly in the back of her mind in those weeks after her return to Paris. But in the front of her mind was her work and the work of the others at the Institute.

She plunged into her new tasks, acquiring a new assistant who was an expert on the management of laboratory animals, helping Bini to design the cages and apparatus for applying glowstone emanations to the rats, and overseeing the welfare of thousands of growing plants in small pots. Some of these flourished and overgrew from the effects of the emanations, and others were stunted or developed strange swellings and burls that baffled the botanists called in to look at them.

She herself often felt fatigued and irritable now, symptoms she had never suffered when Paul was alive. She seemed to need more sleep, and she began to drink coffee to fight this persistent drowsiness. Small cuts and scratches on her hands didn't seem to heal as fast as they had before, and she had a persistent pain in her back that was probably only liver trouble. When it occurred to her that these minor but annoying symptoms had something to do with her exposure to glowstone emanations, she rejected the idea vigorously.

As a matter of fact the others in the laboratory seemed to be affected by the same vague malaise that she was. They were often absent from work, they complained of this unimportant ailment or that, they quarreled with one another and would probably have quarreled with her if they hadn't been so awed by her. Bini mooned about his work, spent a good deal of time smoking cigarettes at his desk and staring into the air, and paid insufficient attention to the rats he was supposed to be observing. The most curious of all was the behavior of Délicienne Maedl, a creature that Claire didn't understand very well. She had always been morose, going about with a continual frown, quick to find fault with the others in the laboratory. But she had carried out her own work with a painstaking diligence, often staying late in the evening when there was extra work to be done. Since Claire's return, however, she had become several degrees stranger. She never smiled and she seldom spoke to her fellow workers; she passed them in the laboratory with a stiff little motion of the head, as though she had a latch in her neck which she snapped in order not to turn her head or smile.

"My dear, aren't you happy in your work?"

"Madame, I am ecstatically happy in my work. How could I not be happy in my work, when I have the privilege of working by the side of Madame? And in an Institute which does so much to serve the cause of mankind? Please do not, Madame, concern yourself with my happiness."

Well? What could one do? Claire's expertise lay in the clean and orderly world of science, where things might be complicated and difficult, but were at least free from the soiled tidal wash of human emotions, which swept back and forth as over a rocky beach, bearing with them all the sorry detritus of mortal passions, regrets, and animosities. There would never be a science of the human soul, Claire was sure of that. The best thing was to pretend you didn't have one. At least then you could get some work done. As an example of its total irrationality, Mlle Maedl's resentment seemed to focus with a particular intensity on Carlo Bini, who was a harmless enough person, anyone could hardly help liking him.

"Maman, who is Mr. White exactly?"

"Who? Oh, you mean Blanco." Claire was a little flustered. "He's nobody in particular, just somebody I met in America. I call him Blanco, and he calls me Claire, but we aren't very well acquainted. It's just the style in America."

"But he brought you to the apartment in his cab. And he helped you with your baggage."

"Everybody's like that in America. In the West, everyone has an enormous respect for women."

"Maman, please don't use the expression enormous respect. I'm getting so tired of it. Did you see much of Mr. White in America?"

"Oh, very little. We had dinner together in the hotel once. And we happened to travel to New York on the same train. You see, Hermine." Claire remembered an important fact, one that had slipped her mind for a moment. "Mr. White, that is Blanco, is really a business associate. In addition to his ranch, he has mining interests in Colorado and owns an immense quantity of what are called Telluride ores. These can be substituted for the Stockhausen earth on which all the work of the Institute depends. And the Stockhausen earth is not unlimited in quantity. Someday it will come to an end. And so Blanco—"

"But he gave you a little dog. And you're so fond of it. You come home from the Institute every afternoon to take it for a walk."

"But Hermine, Boris is a living creature, not just a toy. He's a sentient being just like you and me, with feelings and affections. Now that I've brought him back to Paris, he has to be exercised or he'll be ill."

"Why did you accept him in the first place?"

"I couldn't leave him in Denver with all those other big savage dogs. They would have eaten him alive."

"But why should Mr. White give you a dog?"

"Business in America is conducted like that. As you sit in the dining room of the Brown Palace Hotel, you see businessmen exchanging all kinds of gifts. Not Pomeranians, of course, but—" How had she got onto this subject? How had she arrived, in the course of only a few sentences, at the point of concocting this complicated lie for her daughter? "Well, they don't, really. But Blanco is an extraordinary man. He's offered us the Telluride ores free of cost, and he's even going to ship them from America at his own expense."

"Why?"

"What?"

"Why is he doing all these things?"

"Because he's an extraordinary man, my dear. I've already told you."

Claire was a little out of sorts. She had hoped to have a talk with Hermine about what *she* had been doing in the weeks she lived in the apartment all alone, but she hadn't managed to get around to the subject. Evidently she hadn't done much, in any case. Mme Lacrosse had said that only the harmless Bini had called once or twice to be sure that Hermine was all right and needed nothing. Her daughter was a deep mystery to her; so innocent and candid in so many ways, as transparent as a clear forest spring, and in other ways so impenetrable. Hermine was no longer a child, that was apparent. She was the age that she herself had been when she came from Brussels to

Paris as a student and lived in a small room in the Latin Quarter. She had never done anything with Hermine of the sort that mothers do with their grown daughters; she had only done the things that mothers do with children, the Punch-and-Judy show in the park or a visit to the doll room at the museum. She sought about for a way she could be more of a companion to her.

"I ought to take Boris for his walk." It was four o'clock on a Sunday afternoon and she had just come home from the Institute. Hermine, of course, having no lectures on Sunday, had been home all day studying and eating raisins and cheese. "Would you like to come along to the Luxembourg? And then we could stop at a café afterwards."

"A café?"

"Yes. I know you don't take anything alcoholic, Hermine, but you could have a cup of tea or a grenadine. I used to enjoy it as a girl. Of course you're not a girl now, you're a young woman. Hermine, you're so secretive. Have your—"

"What?"

"Your époques—"

"Oh, Maman." She was eighteen and had had them for five years. What Claire wanted to know, of course, filled with a spasm of quite irrational panic at having left her child alone for several weeks in the most sinful city in Europe, was whether they were still going on. But it was ridiculous! What on earth was she dreaming? It was the sheerest night-wanderings of the mind, old wives' tales, dark mumblings of hags, myths of parthenogenesis, mares inseminated by standing with their tails to the wind, maidens possessed by incubi or hypnotized by unprincipled followers of Charcot. She was astounded at the way this primitive fear had invaded her, trampling over all her reason and her training as a scientist. Hermine was a little strange, but she was a good child, dutiful and trustworthy. And after all, she thought, calming herself, with all these people looking after her, Lancelot, and Mme Lacrosse, and Bini. She charmed everyone, that was the fact of it, and this both disquieted Claire and gave her a secret satisfaction. Her bright eyes, her captious mop of hair, her sly and knowing little smile! Thinking of the pleasure Hermine would take in going to a

Paris café for the first time in her life, she felt all at once a glow of warm maternal affection for her.

At five o'clock on a Sunday evening the Boulevard St.-Michel was crowded with students, some solitary and lonely with pinched faces, and some in groups like herds of alpacas, singing, laughing, and throwing scraps of poetry to each other over the heads of the others. Horse cabs threaded their way through the crowds crossing the street, and an occasional motorcar trundled by with its characteristic coughing sound: Teuf-Teufs the Parisians called them, with their penchant for attaching a nickname to everything, and particularly everything new.

In the Café Soufflet, at the corner of Rue des Écoles, Claire sat at a table with Boris on her knees, and Hermine sat across from her, looking out through the glass at the boulevard. In front of Claire was a glass of white wine, and Hermine had a grenadine with soda; everything was exactly as Claire had planned. She believed all this to be what Hermine had wished, and Hermine almost convinced herself of this too. She watched the people passing, envied the flocks of carefree students, and contemplated totally without pity an old beggar woman who was going through the café with a dirty hand out for sous. The beggar woman was expelled by a waiter; Hermine witnessed this too and saw it as a story, neither a tragedy nor a comedy, simply something that happens in the world, and it interested her deeply. Her mother, she was sure, didn't have this way of looking at things. What would the beggar woman be for her? A social problem to be solved through reason and science? A tumor to be removed surgically? Perhaps an object of compassion who should be taken care of, although it struck her that with all the fine qualities her mother had, intelligence, nobleness of purpose, self-sacrifice, diligence, indifference to pain and discomfort, compassion was not one of them. The beggar woman, out on the pavement, stuck out her wavering chin at the waiter and then turned and shuffled away as the two women watched.

"The poor creature," Hermine murmured experimentally,

not really believing in the adjective herself but curious to see how Maman would take it.

"Such people only spread disease. One woman like that can give typhoid to a dozen people in a week. Such creatures should be kept from contact with the rest of the population. That's what we have poorhouses for."

"I don't think there are such things as poorhouses anymore, Maman. I wonder where she lives."

"Under a bridge, no doubt. One can't really worry about such people."

Hermine wasn't worried, just curious. She went back to watching the people going by in couples and clusters on the sidewalk in front of the window. Occasionally there was a single person, almost always a man. Examining one of these to see what he was doing alone on the boulevard on Sunday evening, she found herself looking into the eyes of Carlo Bini. He had been coming along in the crowd with the others, about to cross the Rue des Écoles, and he had stopped to glance into the window of the café. Playfully and a little maliciously Hermine waved for him to come in.

He pushed open the door of the café and entered. Their glances met again. Claire hadn't yet noticed him, but Hermine offered him a brilliant smile.

"Good evening."

Claire looked up, startled. "Why, Bini. What a pleasant surprise. Won't you join us?"

Carlo sat down at the table. He had left his melon-hat at home this time and was wearing a flat cloth cap like an English workman. This he put on the fourth chair. Then he smoothed his hair, looked from one of them to the other, and smiled without saying anything.

"Of course, you and Hermine are good friends now."

A little of his smile disappeared. "We are?"

"I believe you were good enough to look in on her while I was away."

He glanced at Hermine. After a pause he said, "I was that good."

Claire plunged blithely on. Hermine had never seen her so

animated. "It's only a chance that you found us here. Hermine has never before been to a café in Paris. It's a new experience for her."

Carlo cheered up a little at this. "A rite de passage," he said with his fine Italian smile.

"You might say so," said Claire. She recognized the term from anthropology and was aware of its implications of defloration and initiation into adulthood. Probably, she thought, it was just a witticism. When someone—someone clever like Bini, because he was clever—said something slightly obscure, it was probably witty or meant to be. She had never had time to cultivate a sense of humor, but over the years she had learned to identify a joke when somebody made one and to react appropriately. She wondered if you could learn clever conversation in the way that you learned algebra or a foreign language. It struck her for the first time that Hermine and Bini were two young people—not the same age precisely, but two young people that one could think of as a couple. This thought she formulated painfully and with care in order not to overstate the thing even in her own mind. When she had first discovered Bini standing before the table she had noticed that it was Hermine he was looking at and not her. Well, why should he look at her? He saw her every day at the Institute. And Hermine was a pretty girl; Bini was behaving perfectly naturally. It was just that she had never thought of him as a man with such tastes.

On being pressed, Carlo agreed to take a glass of vermouth. He sipped it and looked out at the passing strollers, with particular attention to the women; when a pair of them went by arm in arm his eyes followed them like a sunflower following the sun. It was a reflex; he hardly knew he was doing it himself. It was amazing, Hermine thought, how people fell into their national stereotypes. Carlo just couldn't help being an Italian Don Juan. Délicienne Maedl resembled the Mont Blanc, a crag unscalable by anyone but an expert, and Lancelot was like his own gentler and more softly rounded Grenoble mountains. Maman, half American and half Belgian. That was a complexity she would have to work out later. And she herself!

No, one didn't want such easy judgments, such neat pigeon-holings, turned on oneself. Half her mother who in turn was two halves, half her father, a genius of science, an absent-minded man crushed by a wagon wheel . . .

Lost in these ruminations, she scarcely noticed what Carlo and her mother were talking about; it was something technical about the Institute. Then a voice from overhead jolted her abruptly from her reverie.

"Good evening, ladies and gentlemen. My compliments, Claire. You must be Hermine, and I don't know who this young gentleman is. May I sit down? I see there's an extra chair. This is probably the gentleman's cap." He handed it to Carlo.

Hermine looked up like a startled rabbit at the tall and rangy American, hat in hand, who swept so easily into the chair and was now looking for a place to set his hat. A waiter offered to take it away, but he refused to part with it and said, "Bring another chair."

"Why, Mr. White—Blanco," murmured Claire, who was just as dumbfounded as Hermine at the sudden apparition of this giant clad in white who seemed to illuminate the whole café with his presence. The waiter came with the chair and Blanco put his hat carefully down on it. He never allowed himself to be separated from it, as if it were the vessel of his private mana. After this ceremony he spoke to the waiter in his perfectly constructed French in which he changed not a particle of his twangy Western accent. "Une Veuve Cliquot, s'il vous plaît, bien fraîche."

The champagne came almost immediately, carried in a silver bucket by the waiter and supervised by a sommelier in a red coat and a key hanging from his neck by a chain. He twisted the wires and expertly nudged the cork; only a little foam flowed out of the bottle. With a flourish he filled Blanco's goblet.

"Won't the rest of you help me drink this?"

"Hermine doesn't take wine. And I don't either, really," said Claire. Carlo opened his mouth and then shut it again.

"As you like." He drank a draught, savoring it appreciatively on his tongue for a moment, and set the goblet down. The other three stared at him silently. "How do I happen to be here, you're all wondering. It's a total coincidence. I just happened to be going for a walk and caught sight of you sitting in this café. I'm staying at the Meurice in Rue de Rivoli but I often stroll in this part of Paris. I like the Latin Quarter. It's colorful. Studios, bookstores, galleries. The bouquinistes along the Seine. All these artists, most of them fake." He waved his hand negligently at the other patrons of the café. "You see more interesting people on the Left Bank. I just met an old beggar woman in the streets."

"Yes, we saw her too."

"I gave her a franc and she almost fainted. She tucked it away in her rags. I asked her where she lived, and she said she had a room at the Angleterre, a quite decent hotel, not far from mine. She probably has more money than we do."

"You don't say," said Claire. "It's odd that you should meet a beggar in Paris, because when I went out of my hotel in Denver the first thing that I met was an American beggar."

"Oh, we have them too, but I'll bet they could learn a few tricks from yours. They don't live in nice hotels, I can tell you that."

"This one called me sister. I didn't care for that."

"Well, he was a Democrat, no doubt. You should have been flattered. He didn't know the first thing about you, but he took you as his equal. No one has really introduced me to Hermine, you know. How do you do, my dear child. I'm Blanco." As he turned, his silver hair caught the light and the points of his suit sparkled like diamonds. He smiled genially at Carlo. "And this is your intended, I imagine."

"Not at all," said Hermine sharply. She had sensed something inimical about Blanco when she first caught sight of him, watching him carry in Maman's baggage from the cab; she had sized him up as a kind of blustering annoyance, an intrusion into her life. Then a few moments ago in the café she had found herself amused by his accent and dazzled by his clothing and person; he made a spectacular effect among the somberer Parisians and appealed to her fascination with the bizarre. Now her earlier judgment was confirmed. She stared at him coldly with compressed lips.

"Oh, I could see right away that he wasn't. I was just joshing."

"I don't care to be joshed. Monsieur Bini is the farthest thing in the world from my fiancé. He's an assistant in Maman's laboratory. I don't have a fiancé and I don't want one. I'd prefer that you'd leave all humorous remarks about my relations to others to a time when you know me better. If in fact that time ever comes."

"Well, I'm sorry if I've offended. I do like a woman with spirit. I like them all, to tell the truth. I'm an inveterate admirer of the fair sex. I even liked the old beggar woman that I gave a franc to. But a man likes different types of women for different reasons. Isn't that so, Bini?"

Carlo met his glance, shrugged, and took a sip of his vermouth. Blanco turned back undaunted to Hermine.

"I like your spirit, young lady. You're like your mother. You've got a mind of your own and you don't mind saying what you think. It may be that you and I are going to be friends."

"I doubt it."

"Although I don't propose to become your fiancé," he went on, ignoring her frozen expression. "I wouldn't care to compete with Bini, a handsome young fellow if I ever saw one. Won't the rest of you help me finish off this champagne? It's a shame to waste it." He fished the bottle out of the silver bucket and held it at an angle in the air, pointing it first at one and then at another. Expertly interpreting this pantomime, the sommelier snapped his fingers at the waiters to bring up more glasses.

"Hermine is only eighteen," said Claire. She was a little out of sorts herself at this abrupt invasion of the visit to the café, which she had planned so carefully as an intimate tête-à-tête with Hermine. First Carlo had barged in and then Blanco, and it had turned into this demonstration of American joshing, if that was what it was called.

"Tomorrow is Monday," said Carlo. "We all have to be at the laboratory at eight."

"It was a pleasure to have you join us," said Claire a little stiffly. "Now we'd better be getting back." She stood up, holding Boris under her arm as though he were a bundle.

The waiter appeared abruptly at Blanco's elbow; before they could object he had paid for everyone's drinks and added tips for the waiter and sommelier. All his money seemed to be brand-new, just distributed from the mint. The silver francs and bronze centimes gleamed like little suns as they slipped from his hand.

The waiter showed them to the door and another waiter opened it for them. A third set of coins disappeared into the hand of the door opener. On the sidewalk Blanco raised his hand, and as if by magic a cab materialized out of the darkness.

"Oh really. We can easily take the omnibus."

"Maman doesn't approve of our riding in cabs," said Hermine with a smooth glance at Carlo.

Carlo said, "My place is only a few steps from here." No one at the Institute knew where he lived, and it was probably a squalid rooming house he didn't want them to see. He bowed, lifted his cap, and disappeared into the crowd on the sidewalk.

"The omnibus—" said Claire again. She got into the cab with Blanco and Hermine.

As it set off along the boulevard Hermine tried to make out her mother's face in the dark, crossed now and then by a ray from a streetlamp. All she could see was a faint and resigned smile. Claire and Blanco were sitting together in the rear and Hermine on the small strapontin facing them. Now and then she caught the gleam of Boris's eyes from her mother's lap. There was a clop-clop from the horse's hooves and a rich, not unpleasant odor of equine sweat. Blanco looked out with interest at the passing shops and houses.

"The Faubourg St.-Germain. There are some fine old houses in this quarter. Most of them date from the eighteenth century, the golden age of French architecture in my opinion. The quarter is mentioned in Balzac."

"You needn't serve as tour guide. I've lived in Paris since I was a girl." As a matter of fact Claire had scarcely ever set foot into this part of Paris except for an occasional visit to a shop in Rue du Bac. She wasn't quite sure why the cab was taking this long way around to go to Rue François-Villon.

"I've often had the notion of buying a house here myself. One of these fine old hôtels particuliers. Or just part of one, an apartment. But I'm quite comfortable at the Meurice. I don't care to cook for myself and I can't stand servants around. Except for the boys at the ranch, of course."

"Why are they all boys at the ranch? Don't you have grown men?"

"Why Hermine, it's just a way of speaking. As you might say, the garçons. Some of them are getting on for fifty."

"What do you raise on the ranch?" In spite of her mild hostility she found herself acting the well-brought-up young lady, as she had with Carlo, and asking him questions about himself. It wasn't hard to do with men, she found; something about them evoked this skill in the feminine instinct.

"Well, generally we raise beef cattle. There's not much market for gazelles, or camels."

"I'm sorry if I'm so ignorant."

"Blanco told me," said Claire placidly, "that it wasn't a business to interest ladies."

"A learned woman like you, I believe I said."

"I stand corrected."

Claire found her mind lightening in the play of conversation. If this was joshing, perhaps she might learn in time how to do it. They were sitting so close together in the cramped space that the side of Blanco's arm was crushed against her own body. For some reason she had expected his flesh to be warm, but the sensation that penetrated through the two sets of clothing was cool, as though it were a special kind of marble, hard as stone and yet tender as a baby's flesh. She tried to move her body away so that a little space would separate them, but without success. There was no question of what was happening; she was driving through Paris in a cab along with a man who was courting her, even though her daughter was along as duenna. She didn't accept the courtship, but he had offered it, and she allowed him in the cab with her. She ought to have been embarrassed and flustered. Instead she found a strange thing in her soul, an impulse to flaunt this amorous exploit before her daughter who now threatened her with her own mature femininity. For Bini had looked at her in a certain way, of that she was sure, and along with her love for Hermine she had felt a stir of primordial rivalry. She grasped for the first time what the point was of mothers and daughters, children and parents. Up to now she had imagined that these terms simply designated parts of a family, innocent figures in a dollhouse of life that remained always the same. Now she saw that it was the coming into being of a child that created the mother, and that the growing-up of the child signified the mortality of the mother. Each generation must age and pass away so that new generations can fall in love, mate, and reproduce in their turn. A shadowy panic stirred in her; but at the same time she felt a deep and almost religious awe of this girl-woman who sat in the cab across from her: the priestess who held in her still childish hands Claire's own fate, the dark story of what was going to happen to her, and the ending of which she already knew.

As for Hermine, this incident of the evening in the café was one she meditated over with a combination of amusement and vague foreboding. She was amused to see her mother forced into the same situation she had been in with Carlo, enticed into a horse cab at night without knowing quite how it happened, and yet secretly pleased that it had happened against her will. On the other hand, this very behavior of her mother seemed to have a parodistic element to it, as though she were mocking Hermine's transgressions while she was in America by acting them out before her eyes. Or even further—Hermine's thoughts plunged blindly on—as though she had brought back Blanco from America precisely in order to have him play his part in this little pantomime, the woman enticed into a cab and driven through Paris in the dark, crushed against her captor, yet not entirely displeased by the events that had led her into this predicament. This was so preposterous that Hermine laughed aloud at it, while still a little wide-eyed with her own panic.

Then another idea almost as ridiculous—no, it was more ridiculous—occurred to her: a suspicion that the chance meeting of the four of them at the café had not been an accident. That her mother and Blanco had arranged this rendezvous, or perhaps that Blanco had suggested that Claire meet him at this time and place, and she had agreed only on the condition that it be made to appear to Hermine a purely chance encounter. How could her mother have connived in such a complicated falsehood for her own daughter? And yet the evidence hung before her like a sword on a thread: Maman's pretense of taking Boris for a walk when in fact it was dark by the time they arrived at the Luxembourg, her coming unhesitatingly to this café when she knew nothing about cafés in Paris, the exact intervals that had elapsed before the arrival of Carlo, then of Blanco, as though it were a scene in a play managed by a director skillful in entrances and exits. She conjectured about Carlo: could his presence too be part of the conspiracy? Further, after leaving the café they had gone a very long way around, through the Faubourg St.-Germain and across the Champs de Mars, while her mother was crushed against Blanco in the dark interior of the cab; it was the best part of an hour before they got back to Rue François-Villon.

And what was the point of it all? It was quite simple. Her mother was having an affair with Blanco, which had begun in America and was continuing in Paris. To cover up this secret, she was arranging for Hermine to have a parallel affair with Carlo. Then, when her mother announced her eventual marriage to the mysterious American, Hermine herself would be so thoroughly involved in this plot from *Les liaisons dangereuses* that she would have no grounds for protest.

Looked at from a point of view more than that of a hysterical schoolgirl, this elaborate story that Hermine had invented to serve her own obscure purposes, no doubt erotic, was preposterous on the face of it. Blanco was a perfectly harmless person, a wealthy American patron Claire had met in Denver. Claire did not agree to meet him in a café. She did not connive with him to make what was really an illicit rendezvous seem an innocent accident. And Carlo had nothing to do with the affair—how could he, since there was no affair to have anything to do with? He had simply come down the sidewalk in his English cap, on the lookout for a girl and hoping to find a complaisant student in a yellow shawl, and instead caught sight of Hermine through the window of the café. As for Blanco, he was a man of absolute honesty, except when he was telling jokes. He liked to go for walks in the evening on the Left Bank, and he was delighted to find Claire sitting in a café with her daughter. He was in love with the one and found the other a charming creature, just the right sort that it was pleasant to josh. The whole thing was innocent chance, pleasant for everyone, except perhaps for Carlo, who played a role somewhere between victim and executioner in this ceremony of innuendoes.

And, to give her credit, even the eighteen-year-old Hermine knew this too. It was not the case that the world existed in order to lay its significance like a sacrifice before her and her alone. It was not the case that everyone in the world was talking about her, pointing to her behind her back, arranging things without her knowledge, joining hands in a silent circle about her. She knew enough of the human mind to know that this was madness. For one thing, she wasn't that important. She did, in a part of her mind, connect this conspiratorial view of the universe to her own sexual awakening, with its new and vivid, mysterious world that had abruptly opened before her. The mere fact of being capable of love, she discovered, makes you seem the center of the universe, makes all these glories the world has concocted seem created for you alone, even when there is no one to love you yet. But she was not at all mad. She was one of the sanest people she knew. She went to the window of her bedroom and swung it open on the chill night. I am Hermine, she told the world silently. I am myself, waiting to be happy and intoxicated with the knowledge that some unknown form of happiness is to come. And the world replied with the cryptic and indecipherable sounds of the sleeping city. Mingled with them she heard a woman's shout in a distant street, the clop of a cab horse's hooves. There was an uneven crepitation in the air, as though the dawn were slowly cracking the darkness of the sky to the east.

On this same night Claire was working in the laboratory late after midnight, putting in extra hours for the time she had lost on her trip to America. It was about a month after her return and a few days after the incident in the café with Hermine, Carlo Bini, and Blanco. She was alone in the Institute except for Délicienne Maedl, who was working in the adjacent refining room, half visible through the open door. Claire was examining a rat that had been exposed to glowstone emanations for several days in the region of his genitals, and she was inspecting these carefully for signs of atrophy or hypertrophy. To do this she fastened the rat to a board while she picked at its groin with a metal probe. The genitals were normal. Later the rat would be bred to see if its offspring in the next generation showed interesting mutations, a phenomenon which had already been observed in the botanical specimens, the milkweed and cow parsley.

She was very tired. It was the fourth or fifth night that she had worked in the Institute until after midnight. She felt unwell and feverish; her back was bothering her again and there were sometimes disturbances in her vision. She ate little and had difficulty sleeping even in the six hours she allotted herself. Sores on her lips, and small cuts and scratches, didn't heal properly. Her menstrual flow had ended, although this of course could be accounted for by her age. All the rest of it too, everything that was wrong with her, could be accounted for by something, overwork, lack of sleep, poor diet, mere coincidence or accident. She still refused to accept the premise that these ailments could have anything to do with emanations from the glowstone she worked with every day in the laboratory.

With care she unpinned the rat from the board where he was fastened and held him in one hand while she opened the door of his cage with the other. The cage, oblong and narrow, was hardly larger than the body of the rat himself. At one end was his food and water, so that the glowstone sample, mounted under the cage to the rear, shone its emanations directly up into his private parts.

One hand on the cage and the other on the rat, she pushed him toward the door and tried to work him into place so that his head would face toward the water tray. She felt a sharp pain in her finger and released the rat, and only a fraction of a second later caught him again. Angrily, and angry at herself for feeling this emotion at a banal laboratory mishap, she pushed him the rest of the way in and latched the door. Then she examined her hand.

There was a smear of blood on the crease of the middle finger, oozing out onto the skin on either side. In the center of the smear she made out a small cut or scratch from which a tiny amount of blood was still welling. Holding her hand to the light and probing at it with the same instrument she had used to inspect the rat, she examined the lesion more carefully. The small red line might have been a crack in the skin from an old glowstone sore, broken open when she grappled with the rat. Or it might be a scratch or bite from the rat himself. If the second, there was danger of tetanus. But that wasn't likely when the cut was bleeding so freely.

She shook off a few drops onto the white paper pinned to the board where the rat had been fastened, and stared at them for some time. At first they were a bright ruby red, translucent and glowing, catching the lights of the laboratory in tiny pinpoints. Then gradually they darkened and grew opaque; their surfaces wrinkled and they shrank at the edges. From liquids they became solids attached to the paper like miniature wax seals. There were six of them, roughly in a star shape, although one was out of place and spoiled the pattern. Perhaps, the idea occurred to her, they were not her blood at all but spots left by the six wounds of the pinoned rat, his four limbs, his head, and his genitals. With an effort of the mind she attempted to draw the red spots, which she now suspected were imaginary, into a perfect hexagon.

She didn't succeed, and when she opened her eyes the spots were no longer there. Her attention was caught by the rat in

his cage, on the workbench a little to her right. Through loss
of blood he had become emaciated, his skin transparent, his
skeleton so reduced that he was easily able to crawl through
the mesh of the cage and out onto the table. She wondered if
she should seize him and put him back in the cage, but this
seemed pointless if he could only crawl out again, and besides
she was a little reluctant to touch him after he had wounded
her hand (she was sure now it was he who had done it). She
watched, fascinated and hypnotized, as he crawled, not like a
rat but like a lizard, to the edge of the bench and toppled over
onto the floor. A bit dazed, he recovered himself and staggered on, plopping down one limb after the other.

And now all the rats in the other cages were escaping, crawling across the tables, and falling onto the floors. But they were
really only skeletons of rats, glassy-eyed and bleached, covered
with thin semitransparent skins like fish skin. They covered
the floor, swaying along and staggering forward in their reptilian manner, staring at one another wide-eyed, maneuvering
around table legs, chairs, and other obstacles like a softly oozing flood, and always making in the same direction, toward
the opposite wall of the laboratory. And out of the wall, as she
watched, came other creatures, wolverines and bats, dragons,
monsters, elves, gnomes, chameleons and salamanders glowing with fire, strange lizardlike creatures with the white saucer
eyes of lemurs, all kinds of medieval monstrosities. Everything
in the laboratory was transformed into something else while
still retaining its original form, and everything glowed.

After these animicula had oozed from the walls, other creatures followed on to join them: pygmies clad as jongleurs;
alchemists, necromancers, and wizards, some wearing pointed
hats, others in medieval capes or robes, or in gowns covered
with stars, some riding on swords, others carrying retorts or
alembics which exuded a glowing steam. They showed these
glass vessels to one another and nodded with emphatic grins.
Then they moved out through the laboratory, still grinning,
bumping into one another and pointing, and assumed their
positions at the worktables, pretending to do all the things that
the staff members did but in parody. With hideous smiles, they

showed each other how to work the centrifuge apparatus. One extracted a bluish stone from his gown, ignited it, and set it into position on the spectroscope, while another chortled with glee at the lines it projected onto the paper screen. A goblin sat at Claire's customary place at the worktable while another, with a chuckle, pretended to be old Bloch, who was long dead now of his ailments, bringing her an imaginary sandwich and serving it to her with a flourish. The Claire-goblin ate it with exaggerated rhythmic motions of her jaw, while the other, grinning, beat time with his hand. One of the alchemists, turning to her in a cunning piece of mimicry, transformed himself into her dead husband, aping his gestures and expression, springing with glee to a bench and pretending to take a reading of the electroscope, holding up his hands to show her his unholy Stigmata. The laboratory was filled with spinning, glowing, silently gesticulating gowned figures, with black shapes, dim stars, glittering obscure objects of glass, bulging frog eyes glowing green in the shadows, a hideous Walpurgisnacht that swam around her with dizzying speed and yet as slowly as a system of planets.

Claire held her hand to her eyes. With difficulty she arose from her place, pushed herself along the workbench (she felt a tiny stab of pain from the cracked finger), and made her way to the door. It opened into the courtyard, and then to the street through a gate in the wall. She didn't bother to close the gate behind her. Outside it was a cold brilliant night without a cloud in the sky; the stars rattled like fragments of angry tinsel.

Délicienne, through the open door of the refining room, observed this precipitate exit of Madame with calm. She too was tired and she didn't have the benefit of worldwide eminence, of many discoveries, of published papers and monographs, to console her for her aches and pains. She was in a strange country where everyone made fun of her accent, comparing her to a cuckoo clock and a yodeler, and she was not considered beautiful. She didn't consider herself beautiful, but in the small town of the Canton de Vaud that she came from this wasn't a matter of importance. Someone married you anyhow and you produced children, who were also not beautiful. Instead of following this time-honored pattern she had gone away to the University of Paris and then to the Savarin Institute, where she had come under the domination of this termagant Queen of the Night, who worked in the laboratory until after midnight and expected everyone else to do the same. And while the others read the scales of elegant instruments, or exposed rats to luminous samples of glowstone, she labored like Cinderella over these caldrons of greenish mud from Transylvania. There was a crew of students from the Sorbonne who were supposed to attend to the drudge work of refining the ore, but they were a carefree and irresponsible lot and couldn't be expected to work at night.

As she passed by the row of caldrons she gave one a kick. The blue flame roared under it and the steam that came from it had a mephitic stench. When she read as a little girl about the exploits of the Savarins in Paris and decided to become a scientist, she hadn't known that it meant passing your whole life amid bad smells. She went to the sink, removed her gloves, carefully washed her hands, and dried them on an unclean towel that hadn't been changed for several days.

She glanced at the clock; it was after two. She went out into the courtyard and looked into the deserted street, where only a policeman's boots rang on the paving stones once in a while. She closed the gate and locked it, and also the door to the laboratory. No one would come to the Institute now until eight o'clock in the morning, when Madame would show up in her black dress and dingy paletot, followed a quarter of an hour later by Lancelot, Carlo, and the others. Inside the building with the door locked she went not to her own refining room but to the laboratory where the others worked.

Everything was orderly and in its place. There was no sound but the muted ticking of the clock and a rustle now and then as a rat stirred in its cage, or a tiny plash as it lapped at its water. The lights were dimmed; the only illumination came from the lamps over the worktables and benches. She prowled

around the laboratory past the various workplaces of her colleagues. Here was Carlo's place. It was rather untidy; the
workbench was covered with papers and there was a rat-dropping on the wooden surface where he examined the animals
and sometimes performed small operations on them, inspecting their spleens or inserting a tube of glowstone under the
skin. Carlo would shit too, she told herself in her expressive
Swiss dialect, if he were dissected alive by an enormous rat
with a scalpel. She derived a considerable pleasure from this
notion.

There was nothing much to see on Carlo's bench or in the
cupboards behind it. She opened a drawer and ruffled through
some papers. Raw data of the experiments on rats, a list of
chemicals to be ordered, a receipt for an English cap he had
bought in a shop. There were some other personal things. She
found a draft of a petit bleu he had sent to that icy little minx,
Madame's daughter. He had rewritten it several times on the
post-office form, crossing out lines and substituting other versions. *Absence your mother from Paris. Reply pneumatically.* All had
gone well with Carlo and Délicienne at first. Matters had proceeded steadily week by week, until one hand had reached a
nipple and the other the clitoris, in a horse cab in the Bois de
Boulogne. Then Hermine had caught his attention and he
dropped Délicienne abruptly, leaving her palpitating and red-
faced after her brief touch of bliss. She had gone back to
laboring over her caldrons. The Prince had tried the glass slipper on her and it didn't fit. They never told these stories right
in the books. She could tell a few fairy tales for them if she set
her mind to it.

She went to Madame's own desk. The Queen of the Night,
as befitting her importance, had several workplaces, one near
the spectroscope, another by the animals' cages, another in the
greenhouse for the plant specimens, and a small office behind
a glass wall where she kept the accounts of the Institute and
the records of employees' wages. This last seemed the most
promising. She found by consulting a large black ledger that
Carlo earned half again as much as she did, and Lancelot twice
as much as Carlo. There was no doubt some justice in this, but

it escaped her. Next to the figure indicating Lancelot's most recent payment, she wrote the word ROBBERY in spidery print, disguising her hand effectively, she thought. She also took for herself some stationery engraved with the name of the Institute. Madame insisted that no one but herself should write on Institute letterheads, but there were many reasons why such stationery was useful, for instance in applying for a job somewhere else. There was nothing much more of interest in the desk. She found a cough lozenge and ate it. Madame coughed, but so did she. If the work of the Institute caused the employees to cough, then Madame ought to provide cough lozenges for everybody free. So much for Madame's office. There was nothing at all at her other three workplaces except, at the table by the animal cages, a few drops of blood on a paper pinned to a board.

The only other workplace of any interest was Lancelot's. In addition to a long and well-equipped space at a table with cupboards, he also had an old rolltop desk in which he kept papers, laboratory logs, calculations, and notes for future experiments. There was an apple in one pigeonhole; he ate one of these daily, not for pleasure but for reasons of health. He also ate stewed figs for breakfast, and had explained to her in great detail why. He all but showed her his specimens. When she first came to work in the Institute, Délicienne had cast a hopeful, or conjectural, eye in his direction, but had ended by dismissing him as hopeless. She was unwilling to attribute his lack of response to her own unattractiveness, since he was no beauty-prize winner either. Neither, as far as she could tell, was he a total eunuch. After a time, through close observation and a little detective work, Délicienne had found the explanation: he was hopelessly in love with Madame, and what was more, chastely so. He referred to her as "our sainted director." Courtly love was supposed to be dead, but he was keeping the corpse alive well into the twentieth century. Oh, he was a prize, was Lancelot.

She went systematically through the pigeonholes of the desk one after the other. She was puzzled by a kind of daybook or journal which he kept, full of mysterious symbols, until she realized it was a cryptographic record of his bowel movements. The symbols were evidently intended to mimic the shapes they represented. This particular day—or yesterday, since it was after midnight now—had not been an especially good one for Lancelot, she noticed. Against the date there was only a small black circle like a nut, followed by two even smaller ones. It was amazing how he kept everything here in his desk at the Institute. Why not at home? Perhaps because this was where the daily event took place. He also kept a record of everything he spent for incidentals, from toothpicks to a needle and thread. He badly needed to be married, Lancelot did. It would cure him of his medieval fantasies, his picture of himself as a knight clanking about defending the honor of a totally unapproachable Queen, and it might cure him of his twitches, his fingernail-drumming and his absent scratches of his head. He needed someone to mend his clothing and keep him in toothpicks, to see to it that he ate his stewed figs, and perhaps it might result in larger and more spectacular symbols in his memoir book. Délicienne was taking a considerable satisfaction in this inspection of Lancelot's rolltop desk.

On to the drawers. There were three of them and they were all stuffed full of things. There were many letters neatly tied up in bundles. She slipped off the strings rather than untied them, since she wasn't an expert of knots and might not retie them the same way. A sampling of each bundle was enough to tell what sort of thing it was. Some were letters from relatives or old school companions, others from scientific colleagues in other countries. Along with them were his own replies; he had meticulously made copies of everything. Lancelot was familiar with English, Italian, and German and was able to read letters in these languages, even though his speaking knowledge was slight. Polylingual herself as a Swiss, she read them with ease. There was nothing of interest in the professional letters. Lancelot had a painful, a pedantic, a consummately boring way of sticking to the point so that there was nothing at all to surprise you in his letters after you had read the first sentence. The letters to him from other people occasionally had an interesting phrase in them. One German

called him a blockhead (Dummkopf in his expressive tongue)
for imagining that glowstone changed itself into lead as it gave
off light, since, if this were true, all the glowstone in the world
would long ago have changed itself into lead. This was an interesting difficulty in the theory and one that Délicienne had
never considered. She made a mental note of it in case she
ever decided to join the other camp.

Finally she came to a little casket, a souvenir of some trip to
Italy evidently, since it was decorated in red enamel with Pom-
peiian cherubs and garlands. In it was some pink tissue paper,
and wrapped in the tissue paper was a single letter. The stamp
was American and the postmark was from Denver. She slipped
the paper from the envelope.

> My dear Lancelot. Words cannot tell how your letter moved
> and consoled me. Solitary as I am, totally alone in the vast spaces
> of this foreign continent, it brought a tear to my eye to read
> your expression of devotion to me and to what we both hold
> dear. And now, the child we have made together I bear with
> me here in America, in this distant land. How many hours have
> we isolated ourselves from the world, in the privacy of our
> companionship, to produce at last this precious consummation!
> The day will come when mankind recognizes this precious boon,
> the promise of salvation for the sufferings and ignorance of
> man. With total affection, from a far land, I am, dear Lancelot,
> your very devoted friend Claire.

Délicienne folded the pink tissue and put it back in the casket, and stowed the casket away exactly where it had been in
the drawer of the desk. The letter she slipped into the pocket
of her laboratory smock. Lancelot, a professor—all professors
are absentminded—would never notice that it was gone. She
felt deeply if not entirely logically that in this way she was
taking revenge on the whole pack of them for the rotten life
she led. Returning to the refining-room, she turned down the
gas flames of the caldrons until their contents only simmered;
they would grumble and fart by themselves until morning when
she came back to tend to them. When she slipped off her smock
in the cloakroom to put on her coat she transferred the letter

to her purse. Then, checking the laboratory to be sure she had left everything in order, she went out the door into the courtyard and through the gate to the street, locking them both carefully behind her.

The chill night air clutched at her through her clothing; it exhilarated her, recalling memories of her Swiss childhood when she was happy with her family and playmates. She strode along the quays in the direction of her lodgings in Rue des Rosiers, careful to keep out of the shadows and under the streetlamps lest some unprincipled person, in spite of her plainness, should attempt to attack her.

Rather belatedly, it occurred to her to wonder what had been wrong with Madame. She had left the laboratory without shutting the door behind her or tidying up her workplace, as suddenly as though she had seen a ghost. She probably had; all she ever thought about was her poor dead husband. Before tonight Délicienne had thought of her as a chaste vestal, consecrated to science and to her private cult of the dead. Now it seemed she had other interests. Délicienne didn't begrudge her this. In a certain measure she sympathized with Madame and the life she led. If only she weren't such a virago. But she shouldn't write love letters to her associates, if they were absentminded professors and left them about in desks.

VI

Claire developed blood poisoning from the small cut on her hand—it was never established whether it was a scratch or a rat bite—and had to spend several days in a clinic at Fontenay-aux-Roses on the outskirts of Paris. It was not serious, but she had to be kept under medical observation while the sore was lanced and allowed to drain. Everyone said she needed a rest anyhow. Lancelot, Delvaux, and the others could make up for her absence by temporarily putting in longer hours at the Institute, and Hermine hurried home from her lectures at the Sorbonne to take Boris for his walk in the park before nightfall. The days were short now in December, and every morning Hermine went out into a twilight Paris that turned first gray and then milky-white during the omnibus trip to the Latin Quarter.

In the clinic, Claire's wound healed more slowly than the doctors had expected. She ran a slight fever and felt restless and unwell. Dr. Simon, the resident physician, puzzled over her and examined samples of her blood. She was run-down, he told her, and should rest more and eat a more nourishing diet—green vegetables, liver, and other things with iron in them. Women her age—he was infinitely discreet about her feminine functions—often suffered from an iron deficiency and this left them anemic and prey to chance passing infections. If she ate a pound of liver a day, he implied, any number of rats could bite her and she would come to no harm. If her blood count was low as it was now, then the slightest scratch might fester and become septic.

She didn't care to eat a pound of liver a day. She lay list-lessly but impatiently in her bed, attended by the Sisters who chatted about her like a flock of cheerful magpies. Her fever caused hallucinations to spring out whenever she closed her eyes, silky images with the texture of mother-of-pearl which were projected on the insides of her eyelids. Because of this she kept her eyes open as much as possible. In this way she got very little rest, even though she lay in bed all day with nothing to do but eat her meals and trail off twice a day with a blanket wrapped around her to the lavatory. She was a dif-ficult patient, the Sisters told her with little laughs.

Lying under the blanket propped on pillows, she held up her hand before her to identify whose body it was that was in bed with her mind. The back of the hand was that of an old woman, sinewy and red-veined, sprinkled here and there with brown liver spots. When she turned it over, the palm was that of a young girl, pink and fresh except for the laboratory scars on the fingers. This was the left hand. The right hand was bandaged and a small rubber tube came out of it to drain the serum from the sore. She ignored the right hand, disclaiming its ownership. When the doctors came to her bedside they could do what they wanted with it. It was painful when the adjusted the drainage tube, but that was a matter for the right hand to come to terms with. She herself had nothing to do with it. She repudiated such a stupid member, first festering from the ef-fects of glowstone, which was good for the health if the hand only knew it, and then allowing itself to be bitten by a rat. They asked her if the hand was comfortable. Talk to it, she told them. The hand had its own pillow, on which it rested next to her on the bed like some precious ornament, a crown jewel or the petrified relic of a saint.

Lancelot came into the room with his hat in one hand and his satchel in the other, tiptoeing as though the slightest sound might cause her more pain. When he saw that her eyes were open he smiled and set his hat down on the table.

"Hello, Lancelot."

"My dear Claire. I hope I'm not deranging you. The Sisters said I might come in at any time. How are you, in fact? I hope they're taking good care of you here?"

"People always ask those questions when somebody is in the hospital. Of course I'm not well or I wouldn't be here. Of course they're taking good care of me. What else do they have to do?"

"And what does Dr. Simon say about your progress?"

"He says that unless I do better he'll keep me after school. I was supposed to stay for four days, now it seems it's to be a week."

"Ah well, I'm sure he knows best."

Lancelot, she thought, always said exactly what was expected; he was a compendium of conventional saws. "Doctors don't know a great deal, Lancelot. They believe themselves to be scientists like us. In fact, they were barbers in the Middle Ages and they've progressed very little since. In the twelfth century they would have done exactly what Simon is doing now, lancing the finger and allowing it to drain."

"Of course much more is known now about sepsis."

"With the result that, now that my finger is septic, they know what to call it. They do have one advantage over us, of course. In addition to being scientists, they are also jailers, and can keep people in rooms against their will."

"Fontenay is a lovely town. In the summer it's full of gardens and roses. If one has to be ill, it's much nicer here than in Paris."

"With luck, I hope to be out of this place by summer. Do sit down, won't you? What's happening in the laboratory, Lancelot?"

He was still standing at the foot of the bed holding the satchel in his hand. He looked around for a place to sit down, but the Sisters had left fresh linen piled on the only chair in the room. "The laboratory is fine. We'll all working extra hours. All the experiments are going forward on schedule, exactly as though you were there. Please don't concern yourself about the laboratory."

And then he went on, saying things that he knew would concern her. "To tell the truth, they all grumble a little, especially when they're asked to go the extra mile. Délicienne Maedl above all. I'm afraid she's something of a disappointment. She showed great promise when she first began at the Institute. But lately she's changed. She seems constantly angry at something or other and does nothing but complain of her lot."

"I've noticed. She's bored and needs a change of work."

"She spoke to me the other day—it was the day after you left, in fact—asking if her salary couldn't be increased. When I said it was up to you, she said, 'If it isn't increased I won't be happy, and perhaps you won't be happy either.' I don't know what she meant by that."

"Tell her I'll pay her another hundred francs."

"I'd rather you told her. And Bini hasn't contributed a great deal lately, either. He feels his research is at a dead end. He'd like to do something else, something more personal—something that would be his own achievement. Perhaps start a search for other new elements in the Stockhausen concentrate."

"Other elements? I don't understand. Lancelot, the Institute was established for the study of glowstone. It exists for no other purpose. What is this talk of other new elements?"

Lancelot found that he was still wearing his hat, which was not good manners indoors. He took it off and set it on the floor by the door. "You see, Claire, these are young people. Just as you and I were young once. They aren't content to follow in the footsteps of their elders. When you and Paul claimed to have discovered a new element in the Stockhausen earth, you were opposed by the entire scientific community. You were young and idealistic then, and you fought for what you believe in. I was the same, when I first joined the Institute. Why can't we give others the same right to be young that we demand for ourselves?"

"Bini can be as young as he wants. He's very young, indeed. But in the Institute our work is devoted to glowstone. It has been since we began, and it will remain so. You see, Paul—"

She stopped and stared at him. "It's stupid. Why did I call you that?"

"Call me—"

"I called you Paul."

The shadow of the dead scientist fell between them. Lancelot grew solemn. "I . . . I've often hoped that you could call me Paul. But perhaps it's best to go on as we have before. It's served us for so many years."

She pushed herself up in the bed, wincing at the pain from her finger. "You see, Lancelot, as I'm telling you, there are changes that can be made and there are other changes that cannot be made. Mademoiselle Maedl can help Bini with his rats if she wants. We can find some other strong-armed person to stir the caldrons. To tell you the truth," she said, "I'm getting rather tired of those dreary rats myself. They depress me and I dream about them. I'd just as soon have somebody else irradiate their tiny testicles."

Lancelot was a little embarrassed at this reference. Remembering that she had told him to sit down, he coughed, stared once more at the chair with the linen on it, set the linen on the floor, and sat down, holding his worn satchel on his knees.

"But the work of the Institute is glowstone, and glowstone it shall remain," she reiterated.

"And if you give up your work on rats to Mademoiselle Maedl, then what will you do yourself, Claire?"

She sighed. The conversation was tiring her a little. "I don't know. There are many things. Perhaps I might turn aside from the work in the laboratory and think a little of the theoretical implications of our research. The discovery that glowstone gives off energy, and that in doing so it changes into lead, has totally altered the modern concept of matter. We've been accused of playing with alchemism, Lancelot. But the medieval alchemists were right; the elements can be transmuted."

"Not base metals into gold, I'm afraid."

She smiled. "No."

"But." He carefully led the conversation into the subject that was on his own mind. "Matter into energy. That's a far more important transformation. The implications for mankind are tremendous. The energy given off by glowstone in the form of heat and light is very small. But a small particle of glowstone will continue to give off energy for a hundred thousand years. Suppose we were able to utilize all that energy."

"We don't have a hundred thousand years, Lancelot."

"If that energy were released in a single instant, instead of over those thousands of years, the amount of energy produced would be prodigious. It would be enough to power all the steam generators of the world, run all the locomotives, provide ammunition for all the armies, explosives for all the mines. Nobel's dynamite would be nothing to it."

She saw that he was right, at least in theory. It was odd that, in twenty years of studying glowstone, this simple deduction had never occurred to her.

"But we have no means of doing that."

"Perhaps one could be found." He gazed fixedly at her. When she made no reply he hesitated, then opened his satchel and took out a sheaf of papers, arranging them on his knees with the satchel as a desk. "I've made some calculations, Claire. If enough glowstone were collected in a single mass, the energy would be released. It would take a kilo or more."

He passed her a sheet with a summary of his findings. She looked at it in silence for a few minutes, then she set it down on the bed.

"But if the energy were released in an instant, the effects would be devastating. It could destroy an entire city."

He nodded.

She threw the sheet onto the bedclothes. "Nobody has a kilo of glowstone. Nobody ever will have."

Here he proceeded carefully, playing his trump card. "Much larger quantities of the pure element would be required, of course. The refining process would have to be expanded tenfold, or a thousandfold."

"But that would not be a laboratory at all. It would be an immense refining factory. It would be prohibitively expensive."

"Perhaps the government might contribute."

"The government?"

"The French government or—some other. If necessary, it could be done in secret, since, if these formulae found their way into the wrong hands . . ."

She picked up the sheet to examine the figures again, and without thinking she took it into her right hand with its clumsy mitten of a bandage. She felt a twinge, and a spot of serum from the drainage tube fell onto the paper. Instead of going over the calculations again she found herself staring at the small circle gleaming like crystal. She closed her eyes, and on the insides of the lids she saw again the Walpurgisnacht-vision she had had in the laboratory late at night, the reptilian rats, the necromancers in pointed hats, the spinning, glowing, and gesticulating figures. She opened her eyes and found that Lancelot was looking at her with an expression of concern.

"Lancelot, we must not even dream of working on this. I recommend that you forget the matter and that you destroy the notes and calculations you've made."

"But Claire. Why?"

"I *direct* you to do so, Lancelot. Give me the papers. I'll take care of them now and throw them away."

"Claire . . ."

"We shall not do this research, Lancelot. Neither will anyone else. You will not breathe a word of these ideas to another human being. They will be our secret, and we too will soon forget them. The conversion of the atom to energy will remain only a theory, something that is taught to physics students. It will not become a plaything of governments."

"A plaything?"

"A weapon of governments."

She was tired and closed her eyes again. She knew that Lancelot was disappointed and bewildered at her decision, but she didn't care. When she opened her eyes again he was gone. Perhaps he thought she had fallen asleep. As she had ordered, he had left the papers behind him on the bed. She would tell the Sister to throw them out. She was not quite sure why she had done what she had done, spoken sharply to her old colleague and companion, and refused him something that was clearly dear to his heart. One thing she knew, she would never have taken such a stand while Paul was alive (but if Paul were alive he would have made the decision, not her!). And in some way she felt that she would not have done it before she met Blanco, that the message that Blanco brought her was a message of life and that the shadow of Paul stood for something else, for darkness. What did this have to do with producing energy from glowstone? She wasn't sure. But she felt strongly that she had done the right thing.

Blanco was an amateur of art in the true sense of the word, that is he admired and enjoyed paintings and supported the arts as best he could to the extent of his considerable wealth. Although he himself had never tried to paint, he had a number of acquaintances among artists in Paris, and he went now and then on weekends to visit a painter friend in the country. He was slowly acquiring a collection of French art which he shipped piece by piece, not to his ranch in Alamosa, where the preferred form of art was pictures of horses in anatomically correct detail, but to a small private museum he planned to bequeath eventually to the city of Denver. In Paris he went frequently to the Louvre and to the collection in the Luxembourg Palace. He particularly enjoyed the Luxembourg collection because it consisted only of works by contemporary artists. It occupied a former orangery to the west of the palace itself, with its entrance in Rue de Vaugirard. These pictures were generally transferred to the Louvre or sent to provincial museums about ten years after the death of the artist, so you had to keep visiting the gallery in order not to be left behind in your grasp of modern French art. This occupied a good deal of his time when he was in Paris.

He was also devoted to music; he went to concerts at the Conservatory and recitals at the Salle Pleyel, and never missed a Wagner performance at the Opéra. Paintings could be reproduced after a sort, through engravings and now photography, but Wagner could not. The gramophone disks that attempted to do so were painfully inadequate, no more than beetle scratches mimicking the heroic trumpeting of an elephant. He had an Edison phonograph at his ranch in Colorado but he didn't bother to buy one in Paris where the Opéra was close at hand.

As for the theater, he sat with a sense of duty, a little bored, at the high-flown neoclassic dramas of Racine and Corneille at the Odéon. He preferred the popular theater in its various forms, especially the Théâtre des Variétés in Montmartre with its vaudevilles, operettas, and other lively pieces. He brayed with laughter at Feydeau's naughty farces, and went with a grin, alone or with some female friend of whom he had a number in Paris, to see the can-can dancers at the Moulin-Rouge. Of course this friend wasn't Claire; he kept her in another compartment of his mind reserved for more serious and exalted matters. Perhaps someday, he thought, he might entice her to the Folies-Bergères, but that would have to wait until he had succeeded in changing her outlook on a number of things, and until her health was better.

In all these spectacles, from the exalted dramas of Racine to the racy revues in the music halls, Blanco never missed a word of the French. His spoken French was excellent too; he was never at a loss for a word, but he made no effort at all to master the difficult sounds that came so easily to native French speakers: the *oeuf* as though someone was hit in the stomach while forming his lips into a kiss, the *mur* which sounded like a cat mewing, the *c* of *tabac* that was pronounced so delicately that some Frenchmen said it was not there at all. Blanco trampled over all these nuances with an easy confidence. *Mur* he pronounced like Muir the American naturalist, *oeuf* was simply uff, and the stuff you rolled up in Bull Durham paper to make cigarettes was taback. Yet because he spoke so distinctly and slowly, and articulated so precisely, he was perfectly comprehensible to everyone from countesses to street sweepers; he had built up a formidable vocabulary and even a total mastery of the more complex grammatical forms, the subjunctive and the conditional. He had no difficulty at all in expressing anything he wanted to in French. However, he preferred to speak English to those who understood it, and even to those bilinguals whose French was better than their English, such as Claire. Like a clever general, he was always to be found on advantageous ground. In English he could utilize the indigenous expressions that came so naturally to him and fitted his twangy Western personality: as queer as Dick's hatband, all around Robin Hood's barn, doesn't amount to a hill of beans. Some of these fell into the hands of bilingual speakers and passed into French: "Ça ne vaut pas un tas de haricots, mon vieux," one waiter told the other at Maxim's, and in a week the expression was being used by half of Paris.

As November wore on into December he continued to stay at the Meurice, in Rue de Rivoli just opposite the Tuileries Gardens, as he always did when he came over for the winter season. It was comfortable, the service was good, and there were very few Americans; they all went to the Athénée up by the Opéra. Blanco dearly loved his fellow citizens in America but not in Europe, where they turned into pompous and trivial idiots, complaining of the plumbing and tittering over the nude statues in the Louvre. The staff at the Meurice knew him well and catered expertly to his needs, arranging for the cleaning of the four white suits he wore in succession and removing stains from his hat with india rubber. He liked his shirts starched and his underwear perfumed with lilac. For breakfast he had a brioche and black coffee, even though he ate ham and eggs in Colorado. Since White was a difficult name for French speakers to pronounce, he was known to the chasseurs and chambermaids simply as Monsieur l'Américain.

Blanco was a great admirer of French architecture and knew the various styles of Paris well, from the Roman ruins in the Musée de Cluny to the modern town houses in the Étoile quarter. He preferred to seek out his architectural finds on foot, and he took many solitary walks to look at houses and public buildings dating from the eighteenth century, the apogee of the French classical style. His favorite part of Paris was the Faubourg St.-Germain, that faded and old-fashioned but still aristocratic relic of pre-Revolutionary days lying between the Institut, the Invalides, the Seine, and the Abbaye-aux-Bois, where he knew all the streets by heart. He often made notes about houses and their addresses in a small red notebook he kept in his breast pocket. It was the only part of his costume, that is the only thing he carried about with him on his person, that was not white, except for his red bandanna.

"You mustn't tell Maman you've taken me to a café."

"Why not? It's perfectly innocent. Think of me as your uncle. Or even your stepfather."

"That's a rather large thought. I'll just think of you as a friend who met me on the street and asked me if I would like a coffee. But we'd better not tell Maman."

Blanco and Hermine had left the café and were walking slowly along the Boulevard St.-Germain toward the University. It was a crisp winter day with a chill in the air, but the sun warmed them a little. A few people turned their heads to look at the student, obviously Parisian, walking along in animated conversation with the white-clad giant in his odd hat.

"You know, I have an enormous respect for your Mama."

"Oh, please don't say that. I've had bad experiences with respect. Any number of men," she said, exaggerating a little, "tell me that they respect me, and the next thing is that they lay their hand on my knee."

"Well, that's a very natural impulse. You're a particularly charming young lady. It's too bad I'm not twenty years younger."

"Oh, don't *you* start." Still she couldn't help being a little pleased. "I thought you were the one person I could trust."

"Well, I can *tell* you it's all right to trust me, but that's a thing you'll have to decide for yourself. It's true that the thing we talked about just now in the café is a rather reckless adventure. If we're going to be fellow conspirators we've got to trust each other."

"I can't imagine what Maman will think."

171

"The address is 27 Rue de Bellechasse. The concièrge is discreet and won't say a word to anyone until the moment comes."

"I really don't want to hear about the details. It's between you and Maman."

"But your Mama doesn't even know about it."

"She'll find out. Please leave me out of it."

"Just as you like. I was hoping to entice you around to look at the place. Since this is a secret from your Mama, it's all up to you. Haven't you ever wanted to make a change in your life?"

"Oh, a thousand times. Not this kind of change, perhaps, but a change. If I were born again—"

"Yes, young girls are always talking about that. But we only get one chance at life."

They had reached Place St.-Sulpice and stopped for a moment by the church. "I did have a previous incarnation."

"Who were you then?"

"Somebody better. Somebody gorgeous and wicked."

"That sounds to me like a dancer at the Folies-Bergères. Someone like Liane de Pougy or Zoë Brooking."

"Are you familiar with such people?"

"Oh, I have a lot of friends of different types. Leaving aside your previous existence as a music-hall entertainer, what would you like to be in another incarnation?"

"First of all I'd like to be a man."

"What a waste, a pretty thing like you."

"Oh, stop. And second, not a scientist."

"You're not a scientist."

"No, but that's what I'm studying at the Sorbonne. I will be one if I'm not careful."

"What's wrong with being a scientist? I greatly admire your Mama."

"Oh, so do I. But for myself, I don't particularly want to be admirable. I'd rather enjoy myself."

"That's all right as far as it goes. But there are a lot of different ways to enjoy yourself. Some are interesting, some seem to be interesting at first and turn out to be just plain dull, and some are quite dangerous."

"Oh, I don't mean abandoning myself to profligacy."

172

"I doubt if you know very much about profligacy. What do you mean then? Let's get this straightened out. First of all, you'd like to be a man, and second not a scientist. Third, you'd like to enjoy yourself doing what?"

"Something—"

"Something?"

"Creative. I want to *make* something. Something beautiful. Perhaps I should be an artist."

"To be any good, you'd have to be making sketches while you were still in your cradle. At your age you'd *be* an artist already."

"Or a musician."

"Same thing."

"Or a dancer."

"They start at twelve."

"Oh Blanco, you're so tiresome. First you ask me what I want to do, and then you say I can't do any of these things. What do *you* think I ought to do?"

"Well, for now, you can just go on being your charming self. You're only eighteen. Later on—we'll have to see."

"You're not much help."

"It's up to you. What are you good at?"

"I don't know . . . just thinking thoughts to myself. They're very interesting, some of them. Perhaps I could tell them to somebody else—"

"You could be a writer."

"Like George Sand. She wrote thirty novels and had several lovers including Musset and Chopin. She also had two babies."

"Did she have a husband?"

"Oh yes. She was really quite bourgeoise. When she set about doing something she always did it properly. First she got married and had the babies, then she met Musset and Chopin."

"Where did you learn all this?"

"At the lycée."

"It must have been a remarkable school."

"It was an international lycée. I also learned about boys there."

"Don't tell me. They pull your hair, snatch your notebook, and pass around pictures of actresses. They also smell bad."

"That's right." She smiled. She really was fond of him; she

had been wrong about him at first. And the idea he had told her about in the café was so generous and would be so—nice for everybody. She had to hurry on now because it was time for her lecture at the Sorbonne. "So I haven't met a real man yet. Perhaps," she said, "it's a shame that you're *not* twenty years younger."

"As you know, my affections in the sense you're referring to are reserved for your Mama. I do respect her enormously. And in order to show my respect for her the first thing I have to do is carry off her furniture while she's away. Will I be able to get into the apartment?"

"Oh yes. I'll be there and let you in."

"What about the concièrge?"

"Oh, Mme Lacrosse. She lets me do whatever I like."

"Still I'd better have a word with her. I'll come by tomorrow then. What time do you get home from the University?"

"About five. It seems very complicated."

"Leave the details to me."

"Men are always telling us to leave the details to them. And look what a mess they've got the world in." She fled; she was late for her lecture.

Blanco arrived at the apartment in Rue François-Villon a little early, before Hermine came home, so he would have a chance to have a chat with Mme Lacrosse. At first she was suspicious, then she identified him as the gentleman in white who had brought Madame home from America in the cab, and they got on famously. She took him into the loge and sat him on a rickety chair by the table. He crossed his legs and was as much at home there as he was at the Meurice, or the Brown Palace. First he praised her seed cakes and drank the herb-tea she offered him, and then he asked her whether she was content with her lot in life.

"My lot in life. For that, Monsieur, what can one do?"

"Or whether you've ever contemplated a change."

"Ah, mon Dieu, Monsieur." She was startled, at first taking this for a proposal of marriage. She knew nothing of Americans, and possibly they were all insane. But she quickly real-